The Story Behind the Story

The book you are about to read is fiction. However, it was inspired by real people I know and events that really happened.

The character of Dio is a combination of several people I've known in my life—especially one young man. They were passionate and talented, but stubborn. I think Dio is representative of a lot of people in the world who were hurt at an early age but always had that special person who motivated them to keep going, to somehow better their lives. From Dio, I learned the unsettling truth of what a young person goes through inside a juvenile detention center, as well as how far a person will go for love and how much a person will risk for true happiness.

Jennifer is also based loosely on a real person—a good friend of mine who always tries to rescue people at the risk of sacrificing her own happiness. She is a totally free spirit who wants more than anything to be how she thinks she "should be," but can never deny who she truly is.

Louise has qualities similar to those of a few special women whom I've met over the years: strong, maternal, salt-of-the-earth types with wisdom gained from hard living.

I have faced numerous hardships in my life and these have motivated me to write about the people and the places you will read about in this book. While this story is a work of imagination, it is closely based on the reality I have known and experienced. I hope reading this story will have the same kind of impact on your life as telling it has had on mine.

—Jeff Rivera

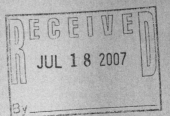
FOREVER MY LADY

A NOVEL

JEFF RIVERA

WARNER BOOKS

NEW YORK   BOSTON

This book is a work of fiction. Names, characters, places, and incidents are the product of the author's imagination or are used fictitiously. Any resemblance to actual events, locales, or persons, living or dead, is coincidental.

Warner Books Edition
Copyright © 2005, 2007 by Jeff Rivera

A previous edition of the book was published by JoAnn/Horatio Publishing and Urbano Book Publishing, 5334 Central Florida Parkway, Suite #180, Orlando, FL 32821.

Warner Books
Hachette Book Group USA
237 Park Avenue
New York, NY 10169

Visit our Web site at www.HachetteBookGroupUSA.com.

Printed in the United States of America

First Warner Books Edition: July 2007
10 9 8 7 6 5 4 3 2 1

ISBN-13: 978-0-446-69881-8
ISBN-10: 0-446-69881-4
LCCN: 2006934324

Book design and text composition by SDDesigns, Inc.

*To anyone who's ever had a dream and
dared to follow it through no matter what.
This book is my living proof to the world that dreams
do come true in real life, not just in the movies.*

FOREVER MY LADY

Prologue

"DON'T BE STUPID, FOO'. DON'T BE A *PENDEJO*."

Dio looked at his homie Spooky's grip on his jacket. Most of his boys called Dio "Playboy" because all the ladies loved him, but those who had known him since he was a kid called him by his real name, Dio.

He took another hit off his joint. He'd given up smoking over a year ago, had to, but on this day he was more nervous than he had ever been in his life.

Thunder rumbled and rain poured, making it impossible to see. Thunder scared Dio, always had. Dio fought to keep from shaking. He couldn't breathe, couldn't swallow. He tried to hide his fear. His mind was set. He had to do it. Dio yanked his arm away from Spooky and pushed the door open.

"Just keep the car runnin', *ése*."

Spooky was a big guy, tattoos up and down his arm and a glass eye. He normally would have just kept Dio from leaving at all, but he knew nothing could stop him. Nothing at all.

Dio jumped out of the car. It was a '57 Chevy, complete with chrome wheels, slick red, with a chili-pepper-hot Mexican *jaina* painted across the hood. Dio had painted that picture himself. It was dope.

He slammed the door shut and looked up at the cathedral in front of him. Lightning illuminated its majestic towers, windows with an eerie stained glass. He'd spent many a night imagining this would be where he'd marry her. They'd have a huge wedding with members of their families flying in from all over the world just to watch this event, this marriage he thought was so destined to be. He'd put his everything into this dream, his one and only dream, and now as he yanked the heavy oak doors open, his heart pounded like a subwoofer.

He dried his soaked clothes with his hand and scratched his shoes on the mat so as not to squeak across the old wood floor. The church was jam-packed, mostly with Mexicans and Puerto Ricans, but some blacks.

Probably his familia, Dio thought. *How could she even think about marrying some* pinche negro?

The grand organ music permeated the building while a choir of children sang, their voices echoing throughout the church. It smelled musty in the air, a mix of wood stain and must as if they had never really cleaned the place, just painted over it.

He tried not to look too suspicious, slipping past everyone. Funny, he was dressed probably better than he'd ever been. Black suit, his wavy black hair slicked back, starched white shirt, polished black shoes.

Dio had grown into a very nice-looking young man. Maybe he could have even been a model, had he played his cards right. Maybe if he hadn't grown up in the slums of Northeast Vegas, he could have been one of those Latin heartthrobs who were in those magazines. Instead, most of the time he looked like the thug most people assumed he was just by looking at him.

But on this day, this very weird day, he was even wearing a tie. Jennifer would have been so proud of him if she could see him. Funny, he'd probably be the last thing she'd see.

He checked his jacket pocket to make sure it was still there. Yep, it felt like a brick pressed against his chest. But he was so numb, or more like so focused, that he was oblivious to it. All he knew was that he had to find Jennifer, and he would use any means necessary.

Wham! Dio bumped hard into a glass table. His thigh throbbed in pain as bullets dropped from his pocket and bounced off the wood floor. The sound echoed all over the lobby. People looked around for the source of the sound, but Dio managed to scoop them up before anyone could see.

He got up and noticed the beautiful ice sculpture on the table—melting, dripping like an ice-cream cone in August. Melting just like his heart.

He saw Father Martínez, his priest, the one he'd grown up with. It was as if the whole world had turned against him. They'd sided with Jennifer, when this was supposed to be their wedding. It was as if she'd slapped him across the face, as if nothing they'd been through together even mattered. The whole thing was surreal.

She loved him. She'd said that over and over to him since they were little kids. She'd taken care of him and believed in him and dreamed with him and held him when nobody else had cared.

"*Estoy aquí para ti.* No matter what—*siempre,*" they'd promised each other. And a promise was a promise.

"Don't be stupid, foo'. Don't be a *pendejo.*" Spooky's scolding remarks kept playing in his head. He warned Dio to just let it go. It wasn't worth it. Normally Spooky would have been all for it, but this time around he said, "*Olvídalo* . . . let it go." It was as if he sensed something was going to go wrong and, no matter how high Spooky had been, his gut was always right.

Dio only hoped this time around he was wrong. He had worked so hard. He could really get a fresh new start now, "a new lease on life," as his probation officer used to say, but now he was risking it all to confront Jennifer.

Was Spooky right? Should he just let it go, face it that she didn't want to be with him no matter how hard and bad it felt? Should he just forget the whole thing? Maybe he'd meet some other *ruca.* Time heals all wounds, they say, and maybe if he'd just—but no. Dio shoved those thoughts out of his mind.

He'd spent the last year changing his life around for her, so they could be together, so he would be the man she said she'd always wanted, so he could be the daddy his daughter needed. They were meant to be together and he was going to make Jennifer understand that, if it was the last thing he did.

He could see Jennifer's family in the front, dressed in their Sunday best. Her mom always made a spectacle of herself with her gigantic summer hat in purple. She never did like Dio and he knew she had probably orchestrated this whole thing, probably arranged the whole wedding herself.

He wondered if perhaps Jennifer was doing this just to make her mom happy, but then he saw her . . . the music changed, the children's choir sounded so beautiful, he had to admit, so irritatingly perfect. All heads turned and everyone gasped as the bride, Jennifer, made her way down the aisle. Her father took her arm, biting his lip, trying not to cry.

He looks nervous, Dio thought.

Jennifer looked incredible. How could she afford a dress like that? *The guy must be rich or something. That's probably what it was. That's probably why she was marrying him. It had to be the money.* The one thing Dio could never give her.

Her gown had a lace top, cut just low enough to show her sensual bustline, but high enough to showcase the first-class act that she was. Her face was shielded by her veil. He hadn't seen her in so long. It seemed like the whole congregation held its breath with him.

Her mom made a dramatic spectacle of herself. Her wails were the only thing that could be heard above the organ playing as the children's choir reached a crescendo, then trailed off. There wasn't a dry eye in the house. Even Dio had to fight the tears.

Thunder rumbled. Her father escorted her over to her groom. He was a nice-looking man, a light-skinned black man. Maybe he was mulatto or something. He wore a striped, stuffed tie, not a traditional bow tie, and the tux must have been Armani or something. He had one of those smiles with teeth so white it blinded you. His gaze never left Jennifer, even as the priest rambled on and on with the vows.

"I, Antonio Estrella—"

What kind of *nombre* was that? Estrella? Jennifer Estrella. It just didn't match her. *No le queda.*

". . . hereby take you as my wife, to have and to hold . . ."

There was a lump in the back of Dio's throat. He wanted to burst out, "No!" It hurt so much.

"I, Jennifer Lalita Sánchez . . ."

He couldn't believe his ears; she was promising him her life. Thunder rumbled and the lights went out. There was a small gasp in the audience, but Jennifer just smiled, the candles illuminating her. She was too lost in the groom's eyes.

". . . to have and to hold, through sickness and health . . ." she continued.

He couldn't help it anymore. Tears came streaming from Dio's eyes. This was too much for him. He was about to explode. His blood boiled.

He looked around at all the stained-glass Bible stories, the creepy statue of Jesus on the cross. He swore Jesus was glaring right at him as if he were saying, "*No lo hagas . . . don't do it.*" He looked the other way, but the statue of the Virgin Mary scolded him as well.

Dio couldn't help but think how proud his own mother had been with how he'd changed his life around, the tears of joy she'd shed. He'd never seen her like that before. He shuddered to think how his mother would feel after all this went down, how ashamed she'd be. Maybe it would drive her to drinking again. Drinking again, after how far she'd come around.

"With the power invested in me by the state of Nevada, I hereby declare you . . . man and wife."

Dio couldn't breathe. The only thing that kept him from passing out was seeing Jennifer's face as her new husband lifted the veil. She was more beautiful than ever. She had olive-colored skin and was the type of girl who never did need any makeup. In fact, she hated wearing it. But this time she was wearing just enough. Her dark brown hair was curled; glitter sparkled in it. She looked like an angel, no, a goddess, better than the pictures Dio drew of her, better than he'd remembered her looking in his dreams.

He'd never seen Jennifer so happy. Not even when she was with him. She had always seemed so distracted, but now she really did look like she was in love.

How could that be possible?

He loved her more than he'd ever loved anyone. *Didn't she see that?* How could she do this to him? The ice sculpture melted like it was on fire.

His heart raced as he reached for the .45 caliber in his pocket, which Dio called his *cohete.* He could hear the rain pounding against the stained-glass windows and the roof. His sweaty hands pulled for it, his heart in his throat. He crossed himself, closed his eyes, and prayed he was about to do the right thing.

Chapter One

—One year earlier—

"YOU GOT COTTON FOR BRAINS OR SOMETHING? MOVE!" THE drill instructor screamed.

He was nose to nose with Dio and Dio could smell the funk from the D.I.'s breath, like cigarettes and garlic. He was a stout black man who resembled a boar more than anything. His eyes were piercing enough to bring an elephant to its knees. His teeth had nasty coffee stains like he brushed his teeth with shit or something and never flossed. Spit sprayed out of his mouth with every syllable he spoke. Dio had a pounding headache from all the yelling and the D.I. had been doing it for the last twenty-four hours, ever since they got off the prison bus.

Dio hadn't had a cigarette in over a week and he was about to jump out of his skin. He's been smoking since he was twelve. He was exhausted, hungry, and just not in the mood for all the bullshit. His mind was on something much more important than all this exercise crap that the D.I. had all the inmates, or trainees as they called them, doing. He was troubled, aching inside, like his heart had been ripped out and stomped on over and over.

It had been over three weeks since he last saw her, since the accident happened. And he couldn't help but wonder if she was okay. He didn't even know if she was dead or alive. They wouldn't even let him see her in the emergency room.

The D.I. had made them run at least five miles so far, screaming in their faces every step of the way, and it didn't look like he was going to let up. And Dio had to put up with a year-long sentence of this?

This wasn't legal. Was it? Dio knew prison boot camp wasn't exactly prison, but they still had their rights as human beings. Didn't they? How could someone make them do all this stuff and get away with it?

Dio could hardly breathe. He felt sick to his stomach and now he had this lunatic screaming in his face like he was some retard or something.

Who did he think he was talking to anyway? Here Dio was, almost eighteen years old, and he hadn't been talked to like that since he was a little kid, and that was from his moms. On the streets everyone had respect for Dio. They all gave him props 'cause they knew he was tight with Spooky and no one fucked with Spooky. They didn't call him Spooky for nothing. And second, they knew Dio would beat them to a pulp if they even looked at him wrong.

You had to be that way in his neighborhood. There was no room for the weak or the lighthearted. They hit you, you had to hit them worse or they'd be treating you like their bitch the rest of your life. The *vatos* in the neighborhood were like dogs; they could sense if you were scared. Dio had seen enough atrocity by the time he was a teenager to make him callous to just about anything. Nothing got to him. He couldn't let it or it'd break him.

He never ventured outside his neighborhood unless he had to anyway, unless of course he was hitting some *putos* in another hood for payback. His favorite time was chillin' with his homies, smoking bud, bumpin' the oldies. But more than that, more than anything, he loved spending time with his lady. His *jaina*, his *ruca*, his *amor*.

Jennifer was by far the best thing that ever happened to him. Just when he questioned if there even was a God, God sent her into his life like a gift with a bow on top. They'd met when they were just thirteen in Clark Middle School. And it was like meeting a long-lost friend. It was surreal. It was as if they'd known each other forever.

Dio remembered that day. It wasn't any more special than any other day he'd had in middle school. It was a typical day from hell for a seventh grader.

"You're not too bright, are you, kid?" asked his language arts teacher, Mr. O'Donnell.

Young Dio sank in his desk as the class laughed in his face. He only wanted to ask a question. He didn't know what a pioneer was. He'd missed so much of class and he wanted to catch up. He didn't think it was such a stupid question.

"Haven't you been paying attention? We spent the last three weeks doing nothing but talking about the Oregon

Trail and you're just now asking what a pioneer is? Should we send you to ESL or something?"

The class roared with laughter. Sure they'd think that was funny. He was practically the only Mexican in the class, except for this skinny, nerdy little girl everyone called Pancake because of her flat chest, but he knew her name was Jennifer.

She was the only one who didn't laugh. Nobody else had to put up with the snide, undermining, racist remarks from everyone every day.

Dio was burning up inside. His eyes squinted and his nose flared. What happened next he didn't quite remember, but when he came to, Mr. O'Donnell was on the floor holding his bloody nose. The next thing Dio knew, he was in the principal's office being screamed at.

Dio waited for his mother to come and get him.

"That's the trouble with you people," the principal said. "We do whatever we can to accommodate you in our classes and what do you do?"

"It's not his fault," a squeaky voice said.

Dio looked up and saw it was Jennifer from class. She pushed her glasses up and rubbed her nose.

"Excuse me?" the principal said.

"It was Mr. O'Donnell. He was saying—"

"There is no excuse for that kind of behavior."

"I wanted to punch him myself," Jennifer said.

Dio looked at her with shock. She'd never said anything to him before. In fact, he couldn't remember a time when she said anything to anyone. Most of the time people "acci-

dentally" bumped into her as she walked down the hall or
threw spitballs in her hair if they paid any attention to her
at all.

"I don't think it's fair for him to get in trouble."

"What are you doing out of class?"

"I walked out."

"You what?"

"I walked out. I told Mr. O'Donnell I didn't think it was
right and he sent me to your office."

From that day on, Dio and Jennifer were the best of
friends. Besides his boys, she was the only friend he really
had. He had to admit he was a little embarrassed walking
down the hall with someone like her, but then he got over
it. Nobody knew her like he did. Nobody liked being with
her like he did. She didn't have the easiest life either, with all
the yelling and screaming in her house. But they'd both hide
away in her tree house and talk the whole night and they'd
eat Rolos 'cause she knew Dio loved chocolate. And she'd
sing to him with the most beautiful voice and talk about
their dreams. They'd sleep there at night whenever things
were bad. They never messed around or anything; their
bond went beyond sex. It was a friendship, a true friendship
Dio had never experienced before.

But then they were separated when his mother kicked
him out of the house that year and he ended up lost in the
foster-care system until he was eighteen. He thought he'd
never see her again, until they were reunited just months
ago after all these years. It was like they picked up where
they left off.

It wasn't just some puppy love for the two of them. No, it was true love, real love that only comes around once in a lifetime, and Dio felt lucky just to hold her in his arms. He felt alive kissing her soft lips, or smelling the scent of her hair when she hugged him and buried her head in his chest. Everything about her he loved.

She was the first one to notice his talent as an artist and encouraged him to go for his goal of owning his own car design shop.

"Nobody will hire me," he would say.

"You won't have to be hired, you'll be hiring them!" she'd respond.

He loved it when she said things like that.

She was the only one who saw him as more than just some thug on the street, some *vato*, some gangsta. She encouraged him; she believed in him like nobody ever had.

He was so much more than the way most people saw him and she knew it. He hated driving down the street and having people lock their car doors as he pulled up. He hated the way they pulled their children closer to them as he walked by as if he were going to snatch the kids right out of their arms. He hated being hassled by the cops every night he went out to chill with his girl for no other reason than being Chicano in a nice car. He hated being judged, period.

Jennifer saw the real side of him, the side he never showed anyone, his vulnerable side. He could tell Jennifer anything and she'd listen. She'd share with him her deepest secrets that she wouldn't dare tell her *familia* and she knew he'd never say a word. They were more than just lovers; they were best friends, and she was by far the only best friend Dio had left. And even that was in question. It seemed like anyone who ever got close to Dio ended up dead or abandoned him. It was like a curse, and now it was driving him loco not knowing if she was okay.

"Halt!" the D.I. said. "I said halt!"

Most of the trainees were about as confused as he was, didn't have a clue what the D.I. was talking about, but they figured he must be telling them to stop. *Thank God. Maybe now they could rest.* He was beyond exhausted. He felt like his stomach, his lungs, and everything else would come spewing out of his mouth at any moment.

The only one who looked more pitiful than him was this skinny mulatto kid the D.I. called Simon. He looked like he'd fall over if someone breathed on him hard. He had to be the nerdiest-looking kid Dio had ever seen. You could play connect-the-dots with the poor kid's zits. Dio hated to admit it, but he wondered, with Simon's Coke-bottle glasses and everything, how the kid could manage to look at himself in the mirror. It was that bad.

"What are you huffing and puffing about, trainee?" the D.I. said, screaming at the top of his lungs in Dio's face. Dio was keeled over trying to catch his breath.

"Looks to me like you're out of shape. Stand up."

"I can't."

"I? Who's 'I'? Your name is Trainee Radigez."

"Hold up, a'ight? Jeez," Dio said.

The words came out of Dio's mouth before he realized

the big mistake he had just made. It was too late. The D.I. came at him like a semi.

"Who the hell you think you're talking to, boy? Who said you could talk to me, trainee? What's the third general rule from your manual?"

Dio was supposed to have memorized some fifty-page manual they gave them the night before with all these ridiculous rules and regulations. But the last thing that was on his mind was reading some stupid booklet.

Dio rolled his eyes and stood up. "I don't know. You tell me."

"You gotta be out of your cotton-pickin' mind. You dying on me, trainee? You better be dying on me if I see them eyes rolling around in your head again. The third general rule is, 'Trainees do not speak unless they are given permission.' You hear me, boy?"

"Yeah, yeah."

"How do you answer an officer?"

Dio shrugged. Drill Instructor Jackson mimicked him. "What's that supposed to mean?"

Jackson flicked Dio's long hair.

"Nice," he said with a smirk on his face. "Are you a sissy?"

Dio was burning up. What was wrong with his hair? Sure it was long; he hadn't cut it since he was like thirteen. Jennifer liked it that way. She always said that was her favorite part of him, that and his eyes. Besides, it reminded him of the Bible stories of Samson that his mother used to read him. Samson never cut his hair because it gave him strength; same for Dio. That strength had kept him alive all these years.

"I asked you a question, trainee."

"Hell, no. I ain't no sissy. What the fuck do you want me say?"

"You're really cruisin' for a bruisin', aren't you, trainee? 'Sir! Trainee Radigez doesn't know, Senior Jackson, sir!' That's what you say!"

"Sir, Trainee Rodríguez don't know, Senior Jackson, sir," Dio answered back half-heartedly.

He just wasn't in the mood for this. He could feel the stares of the other trainees. He hated when people stared at him.

Senior Jackson cupped his ears, "What? Say that again. There something the matter with your voice? I can't hear yooooooooou!"

"Nooooo, there's nothin' wrong with my—"

Jackson shoved his finger at Dio's head.

"Think, trainee, think."

If he touches me one more time . . .

"Goddamn, you're a slow learner. Are you a slow learner, Trainee Radigez?"

"Sir, it's Rodríguez, sir. Not Radigez."

Jackson stepped up to Dio like a train about to hit a car on the tracks. "You correcting me, boy? You don't speak until spoken to, you don't shit 'til you're told to, and you don't eat, sleep, or breathe unless I tell you to. Do I make myself clear?"

"Yes . . . sir, yes, sir!"

He cupped his ear again. "What? I can't hear you, trainee. There are no secrets here, trainee. Speak up!"

"Sir, yes, sir!"

Dio hated repeating himself and he hated even more having to speak up when he didn't feel like it. Everyone was staring at him as if he were an idiot, worse yet, as if he were some bad kid in the classroom who just got in trouble. It brought back too many bad memories.

Jackson looked Dio up and down, heaving and huffing. He let out a little laugh. "You look like an ignoramus. Are you an ignoramus, Trainee Radigez?"

What the hell was that supposed to mean? Dio wondered. It didn't sound good.

"Sir, no, sir."

Jackson turned to the other trainees. "Does he look like an ignoramus, trainees?"

They looked at one another trying to figure out what the hell he was talking about.

"Look at me, dammit! I asked you a question!"

They obeyed and answered back with a mish-mashed version of "Sir, yes, sir!" and "Sir, no, sir!"

Jackson laughed in their faces. He gave them the once-over, pacing in front of the line one step at a time. They were all wearing dark shirts, the sign of a beginner in the camp.

"You got three levels to get past in this camp and half you faggots won't make it past the first one."

He flipped through the pages of a clipboard and shook his head.

"You don't know what it means. Do you? Do you?"

"Sir, no, sir!" they answered.

"So I got a bunch of dummies here. Oh, great. Hit dirt and give me fifty."

They looked at one another as if looking for some clarification.

"Now!" and they dropped like flies, giving him pushups.

Dio couldn't believe it. Couldn't he see they were exhausted as it was? Why was he making them do more?

This was stupid.

"There is no fun here. If you're not working, you're in school studying. And every night if you're not in your bunks sleeping, you're reading the dictionary. Each of you will be provided a copy of it and I expect you to know it backward and forward along with your general rules. The next time you don't know a word I want you to look it up in the dictionary. And you better know what it means, next time I ask ya. I expect every single one of you to know the meaning of *ignoramus* by tomorrow. Do I make myself clear, trainees?"

They stuttered, then coughed up, "Sir, yes, sir!"

"What in the hell was that? You sound like a bunch of pansies. Are you a bunch of pansies, Trainee Grossaint?"

He stepped in front of a white kid with ice-blue eyes and chiseled features, diligently doing pushups as if he were reading a book.

"Sir, no, sir!"

"You sure about that, Grossaint? 'Cause you all sound like a bunch of pansies. So, we got a bunch of pansies and dummies. Great combination."

Dio felt sick to his stomach. He felt as if he were going

to cough up his lungs at any moment. He could barely handle the five pushups he had done already and he had forty-five more to go? His body quivered with each pushup.

Jackson bent over and got into Dio's face, "What kind of pushup is that? That's not even a girl pushup."

The trainees chuckled, which burned Dio up.

"I'm . . . sir, I'm . . . Trainee Rodríguez is trying, sir."

"Trying? What the hell does that mean? Trying? You either do it or you don't. You are a pathetic excuse for a man if I ever did see one."

Jackson stuck his weathered boots under Dio's chin.

"When your chin hits these boots, then that's a pushup. Start over . . . one . . . two . . ."

He says one more word, one more word . . ., Dio thought.

He would have done something about it right then and there, but now he was feeling sicker than before. It could have been the dung smell of Jackson's boots, could have been the exhaustion, could have been anything, but when it happened, Dio had never felt more embarrassment in his life. His last meal and about everything else he had in him poured out of his mouth in chunks right on Jackson's shoes.

"What in the hell? Get up, trainee! Get . . . up!"

Dio struggled up.

"I can't believe this!" Jackson went on. "You sick or something, trainee?"

"Sir . . . no . . . sir."

"Then why the hell . . . ? You're out of shape; that's what your problem is. And you probably want a cigarette, too. Would you like that, trainee? Would you like a cigarette?"

"Sir, yes, sir."

"This look like a quickie mart to you, Radigez? Grossaint, get over here."

Grossaint hustled over to Jackson's side. "Sir, yes, sir!"

"This look like puke to you, Grossaint?"

"Sir, yes, sir."

"Why is there puke on my boots, Grossaint?"

"Sir?"

"Don't make me repeat myself, Grossaint. That really ticks me off."

"Sir, 'cause Trainee Radigez—"

"No! No! And no, Grossaint! There's puke on my boots 'cause you haven't cleaned it off yet. Get on down there and clean it up."

Grossaint dropped to his knees. "Sir, how do I—"

"You got a shirt, don't you?"

Grossaint grimaced. He gave Dio a look of disgust and took the lower end of his T-shirt and began to clean it up while still wearing the shirt.

What a smell.

"Hurry up, we got a lot to do. And I want to see myself in the reflection by the time you're done. Hurry up, Grossaint."

Grossaint worked hard at the shoes, scurrying after Jackson as he approached Dio. Everyone watched in shock. Dio couldn't have been more embarrassed, but he kept up his façade.

Jackson stood in front of Dio, nose to nose, and for the first time said something in almost a whisper. "How you feeling now, Radigez?"

It was not what he said that bothered Dio the most, but the way he said it. All that could be heard was the trainees catching their breath and Grossaint scrubbing at the shoes. Jackson's intense dark eyes peered right through Dio's soul, but he lifted his chin in a defiant stance.

"I said, how you feeling now, Radigez?"

"Sir, fine. Feeling fine now, sir," Dio answered back, never looking away.

A smile curved on Jackson's face as he stared Dio down. "There is no competition here, Radigez. No challenge to overcome. One way or another, you're going to learn. I will win. I always do."

He resumed his normal top-of-his-lungs resounding voice.

"One of you fuck up, you all fuck up. Understand?" Jackson said. He looked right at Dio as he said it.

"Sir, yes, sir!" the trainees answered back.

"You done yet, Grossaint?"

"Sir, yes, sir!"

"Get up then and get into place. Take your shirt off, Grossaint. What's wrong with you?"

"Sir, yes, sir!" Grossaint answered.

"Seems to me Trainee Radigez is tired, so you're all going to have to do the running for him. Five more miles."

They couldn't believe it. Dio could feel their cold stares on the back of his neck.

"Now!" Jackson commanded.

"Sir, yes, sir!"

"You just sit there and relax, Radigez. Sit there and enjoy

yourself. Don't worry," he said with a crafty smile, "they'll take care of everything."

Bzzz! Dio couldn't believe his eyes. Almost five years' growth fell on the floor as a junior officer shaved off his hair. Clump after clump it fell and Dio did whatever he could to remain strong. He wasn't about to give them the pleasure of seeing how the haircut was tearing him apart.

If Jennifer could see him now, she'd be shocked out of her mind. His mother hated his long hair; in fact, it seemed like she hated just about everything about him. His hair was his strength. He felt, with every clump that fell on the floor, that he was getting weaker and weaker. He held on to what little strength he had left.

It was times like that, in camp, that he wished Jennifer were around. Dio had loved lying next to Jennifer late at night after he'd snuck into her bedroom. And they'd whisper and laugh all night long, knowing if her parents ever found out, they'd have him arrested. They never did like him. They never understood the special thing he and Jennifer had together.

They were probably jealous, Dio often thought.

Her parents' love had long ago fizzled out. They were like cold tamales that used to be piping hot.

He glanced at the twenty pairs of eyes staring at him. It seemed like all the trainees had already paired off into cliques. It was as if he were in junior high again and nobody wanted to be his friend.

Dio felt completely naked as the last clump of hair fell to the floor. It felt weird as the breeze flowed through his almost bald head with every step he took. He tried to keep his head up, walking past the glaring eyes of his fellow trainees as though he didn't know that they were staring at him.

He could see Grossaint's eyes following every move he made as he found an empty spot on the floor and sat down, alone. He'd only been here for a few days and already he'd made enemies.

Dio's eyes met Grossaint's ice-blue ones. He couldn't figure Grossaint out. He had one of those faces that said a lot, but you didn't understand the language. It was like looking through a big dictionary and not knowing where to start. Grossaint just looked at him as his friends whispered things in his ears: Dio imagined that couldn't be a good thing.

Dio was beat by the time they got into their tent. It was a large tent with bunks sitting on the hard desert ground. Nothing's colder than the February winter in Las Vegas. It's the type of cold that just clings to your bones and rattles them. Dio had slept on floors more comfortable than those bunks, but at this point he felt like he could sleep on just about anything.

It was only 8:00 PM and they were already ordered to go to bed like they were six-year-olds or something. Dio tossed and turned on his bed, switching the so-called pillow over and over trying to get a more comfortable side. His mind was troubled. He was living in hell and there was no way out. Hell on the outside and riddled with guilt from the hell inside his head.

His mind was filled with questions and worries about Jennifer. He wondered if she had died on that hospital bed or, if she was alive, if she was in pain. If she was still alive, she probably wondered what had happened to him and probably wanted to know why he hadn't contacted her at all. Maybe she was just as worried about him. He wanted to be near her so badly. She was the only thing that kept him sane in that crazy gangsta life he led. If he could just get to a phone, just for five minutes. He just needed to hear her voice again. Just needed to know that his baby was all right.

Every time he tried to go to sleep that night, everything that had happened would play in his mind over and over again.

Dio remembered standing outside Miguel's Mexican Restaurant that night on East Charleston, on the pay phone with the rain coming down in sheets. He had planned to go home real quickly before he spent that Valentine's evening with Jennifer. It was supposed to be such a special night, but it turned out to be a horror instead.

He was an emotional wreck because his mom had just kicked him out once again. She was pissed because he had gotten arrested for beating up a couple of punks. *Didn't she understand? She would have done the same thing in the same situation.*

By then he just wanted to get out of Vegas completely. He knew Jennifer was right. He'd been part of the Paisas gang sect since he was thirteen. They were his boys and practically the only real family he had besides Jennifer. As soon as he got jumped in the gang, Spooky had taken him under his wing when nobody else would. But he had to get out of the gang if he and Jennifer were to have any type of normal life together. She told him that over and over again and he knew it. But this time, he was going to do something about it. He had convinced her to give up everything she had going for herself, even her repaired relationship with her *familia*, to run off with him to L.A. where they could both start over. She didn't want to, Dio knew that, but she loved him enough to do it anyway if it meant they could be together.

He knew how troubled she was that night, so quiet. He knew she was thinking about all that she was leaving behind, even the new gig she had just got at the Palms Hotel as a backup singer. She loved him that much. And he promised her that things would get better once they moved to L.A. They were just minutes from the state line when it happened. Those damned potholes. With a city as rich as Las Vegas, it was amazing that they even had potholes in their roads. If only they hadn't gotten that flat tire. If only they hadn't gotten out to fix it.

Sometimes Dio wondered if God was teasing him or something. Like God would toy with him, give him something nice, like a piece of yarn to a kitten, then snatch it away just when he thought he had something good. Couldn't he ever have something as good as Jennifer? Didn't God know

Dio was going to turn his life around that night? He was going to leave all his homies, *la vida loca,* behind. He was going to start over again. *Didn't God see that?*

Dio shook his head, tried to get that awful night out of his mind. He got down on his knees and said a prayer, just like his mom had taught him to do every night since he was little. Then he crossed himself and hopped back into bed. His mind trailed off, about to slumber off when it began . . . the whimpering. It started out just as whimpering, then crying, then sobbing, loud sobbing. Dio tossed and turned.

"Shut up!" the trainees yelled.

It was Simon, that nerdy kid, crying up a storm. It was the second night in a row and Dio was ready to kill him.

What the hell was he crying about? Dio wondered.

He went on like that for hours, all night long. And just as they finally got some sleep, Senior Jackson was in their face screaming at the top of his lungs, "Rise and shine, Radigez! There's work to be done!"

Dio always hated gym class. Sure, he loved sports. Or at least he pretended to. Isn't that what all guys were supposed to love? Sports? He cared more about hanging with his homies and drinking than the actual game. And now it was like he was stuck in never-ending gym hell. Every morning they did one hundred pushups, two hundred sit-ups, at least two miles of running, and whatever else Jackson could think up. And that was before their breakfast, or "chow," as Jackson called it.

Then they'd begin their daily chores. That day Jackson decided to subject them to cleaning the whole inside of the main building—the walls, the ceilings, the floors, the cracks, and the corners—all with a toothbrush.

"I want to see myself in the reflection," he said.

They started working at eight in the morning and didn't finish until about 3:00 PM. Dio's shoulders were aching. His knees were raw from scrubbing the floor and his neck was throbbing from being hunched over for so long. His whole body ached, but his mind was on Jennifer.

They were just about to finish up when Senior Jackson came around for a checkup. He whistled as he checked every nook and cranny he could find for dirt.

He walked past Dio, who pulled the pail of dirty water closer to him so Jackson could walk by. Everyone froze as he walked by, but then he stopped right beside Dio. He smelled the air, looking every which way. Everything looked as clean as could be.

Jackson was about to step away when Dio cleared his throat.

"Um, sir, Trainee Rodríguez requests permission to speak, sir," Dio said.

"What?"

"Sir, Trainee Rodríguez was wondering if he could . . . use the phone for just a minute or two, sir."

A laugh came from Jackson's belly and made its way up through his mouth.

"You are asking me for a favor, Radigez? You are asking me for a favor?" Jackson chuckled some more, making Dio feel like complete shit. "What's the sixth general rule, Radigez?"

"Sir, the sixth general rule is to, um . . . trainees must earn their privileges. But, sir, I'm . . . Trainee Rodríguez is trying to find out if my . . . his girlfriend is okay, sir. She . . . Trainee Rodríguez don't know if she made it out of the hospital—" His voice cracked with emotion.

"No!" Jackson belted out. "You want phone privileges, you gotta earn them."

"But, sir—"

Jackson kicked the dirty pail over and down the hall. He even splashed it on the walls.

"I said I wanted it clean, Radigez. Everyone do it over— all of it. You fuck up one more time, Radigez, and it's on you and you alone. Nobody's getting in trouble 'cept you."

And with that he walked off, mumbling something about if he let Dio use the phone, he'd have to let everyone else. Everyone groaned until one of the junior officers told them to shut their holes.

Dio could feel the haters on the back of his neck. They didn't dare say anything, or the junior officers might do something about it. But it was as if Dio could read their minds. They weren't happy and it was all his fault.

Jackson had a vendetta against him and it seemed he was determined to make his life a living hell, worse than it was already.

Didn't he care about anyone? There had to be a heart somewhere deep inside him. Even he had to show some kind of compassion.

Dio felt like he was going to go crazy until Grossaint crawled up next to him, careful the junior officers didn't spot him.

"He's a jerk," Grossaint consoled.

It had to be the first time Grossaint had ever said anything to him and Dio didn't know what to make of it.

"We should be able to use the phone any time we want," he continued.

Was Grossaint actually trying to make friends? Maybe he was. Maybe he wasn't as bad a guy as Dio had thought.

"*Simón*," Dio whispered. "It's inhumane, that's what it is."

"No kidding. What? You gotta call your girl or something?"

"Yeah, man. I think she's still in the hospital. I don't know."

Grossaint nodded toward Jackson's office. The door was slightly open. "You oughta just go in there and use the phone."

"No way, man."

"No, I'm serious. We got your back." Grossaint eyed the junior officers, stepping away from their presence. "Go now before they get back."

Grossaint was right. If he was going to do it at all, now was the time. And even if he did get caught, how bad could it be, anyway? He'd just make them do more pushups or something. It was worth the risk. Jennifer was worth every bit of freedom he had left. Besides, he'd just be making a quick phone call anyway.

Dio nodded, checked to make sure the officers still weren't there, and stepped up to the door. Grossaint gave him a reassuring nod as he snuck into Jackson's office.

His heart was pounding a million times a second. He scanned the office for the nearest phone, but the desk had mountains of paperwork and files everywhere. For someone who insisted they have neat and tidy quarters at all times, Jackson's place looked like a pigsty. Dio ducked below his desk and fished for the phone. Just pictures of what looked to be Jackson and his son, the sports page, an empty box of nicotine patches, and . . . then he found it, the phone, underneath some folders.

He grabbed the phone and yanked it under the desk with him. He checked for another reassuring nod from Grossaint that the coast was clear and began to dial. Busy signal. He had to dial a 9 to get out, so he did.

"Four-one-one."

"Clark County Hospital," Dio whispered.

"I'm sorry, sir. I cannot understand you," the operator said.

Dio repeated himself more sternly. "Clark County Hospital. Hurry up."

Dio dialed 1 to get it to directly connect. His heart was in his throat by this time. He just needed to know, to hear her voice, to know she was still alive. If anything happened to her, Dio would never forgive himself. She'd been by his side ever since he was a teenager. She'd been loyal even when her parents did whatever they could to pry them apart. She stuck up for him and always had his back, a lot more than most of his homies ever did, even Spooky. Dio knew that Spooky was like a big brother to him, but if it ever came down to the wire and it was between his life and Spooky's, Spooky would save himself first. But Jennifer, she'd take a bullet for him.

"Hello?" the voice answered.

Dio snapped out of his daydream. "Yeah. You got a patient named Jennifer Sánchez there?"

"One moment."

Seconds felt like hours, his throat was dry, his breath labored.

Please, please, God. Please let her be okay. Please let her be okay.

"I'm sorry, Ms. Sánchez—" the receptionist began.

Dio's heart dropped.

"Oh, wait a minute. I'm sorry. That was a different patient. Yeah. Please hold."

What's that supposed to mean? Dio wondered.

The phone rang again and Dio checked to make sure no one was looking. He couldn't see Grossaint, but guessed everything was okay.

Some guy answered the phone. "Hello?"

"Yeah, Jennifer there?"

"Who is this?" the guy asked.

"Who is this?" Dio insisted.

"Oh, I'm . . . hold on."

It must have been some male nurse or Jennifer's relative or something. Dio let it go from his mind. A bunch of rustling noises and muffled speaking voices was all Dio heard. Then it came, her voice dry, weak, and quiet.

"Hello?"

Dio was like a little kid again, talking faster than his mind could keep up with.

"Jennifer, baby. You're all right. Oh, my God. I've been so worried about you. I wanted to reach you, but I'm in this camp, this prison camp, and they don't let me do nothin'. And all I've been thinking about while I've been here is you. And I've been praying, Jennifer. I've been praying every night since I last saw you that you'd be all right. Baby, I miss you so bad. Are you okay?"

She didn't answer right away, which only made Dio more worried. "I'm . . . I'm okay. Got shot six times."

"I know, baby, I know."

"I'll be in here for a while."

"How long?"

"At least another three weeks, they say."

"Baby, you stay strong, okay? Any moment I get to call you I'm going to. I'm not supposed to be using the phone right now, but I needed to hear your voice. Baby, if I could be near you right now . . . I wanna hold you and kiss you and make sure you're all right. You know that, don't you?"

"Dio—"

"Baby, you know I'm so sorry about everything that happened. You saw I tried to take the bullet for you. Didn't you? You know I wasn't about to let those *putos* get to you, right? You know it's not my fault, right?"

Again she didn't answer for a long time. It was like it was painful just for her to think.

"Dio, we need to talk," she said, her raspy voice slow and faint.

"Baby, you shouldn't talk now. You need to rest. I won't keep you on the phone. I just needed to hear your voice. And now that I know that you're all right—"

"Dio!" she said sternly. Her tone shocked him.

"What's wrong, baby?"

She paused for a while and Dio wondered what was going on in that room that was causing her not to answer him right away.

"You know I care for you, don't you?" she asked.

"Of course. You care for me. And I care for you, baby. You know that."

"Dio, we'll always have a connection. I told you that before, but . . . you gotta get some help."

"What do you mean? Baby, I'm straightening things out. You'll see."

"Dio. You and me—it's . . . I'm sorry, but it's over."

Dio couldn't speak at first

"Dio? Dio? You there?"

"It's just your medication talking right now," he finally said. "You should rest."

"No. It's not my medication, Dio. It's—"

"What? What are you saying, baby?"

She was crying now. "I'm sorry, but I can't live like this anymore, Dio. My *familia* is right. I can do better. I've got to do better for myself."

"Baby, we're soul mates. You can't just . . . I need you. Don't you see? The whole reason I'm even in camp right now is 'cause of you. You can't betray me like this."

"Dio, I'm not betraying you. Don't try to twist it like that. Just try to understand. 'Kay? I . . . I got to go now. Just please understand."

Click. Nothing but dial tone permeated the air. Dio was in a state of shock. Now, for the first time in his life, he felt like his whole world had shattered completely, like he didn't have a friend in the world. He was alone. He was actually alone. Not even God wanted him, it seemed. Dio's nose pinched. He could feel the tears starting to well up.

It was impossible. He must be dreaming. He had to be. Jennifer would never give up on him, not his baby. She'd been there for him always. There was no way she's just drop him like a . . .

"What the hell are you doing in my office?" Jackson hollered.

Before Dio could get out of the way, Jackson had him by the collar and lifted him out the door and down the hall so fast Dio didn't know what hit him. He looked back at Grossaint, who had a crafty smile curved up on his face.

Chapter Two

DIO SPENT THE NEXT FOUR DAYS IN A PRISON CELL, NOT knowing what was going to happen to him. He'd never been in an adult prison before, let alone in what they called the "hole." It was solitary confinement, as dark as night, and for Dio, someone who had memories of being locked in a toy box by his mother whenever he was "bad," it was claustrophobic hell. He'd never seen his mother do it to his little brother, Daniel, but he feared what went on when he was not around.

No matter how much water they brought him in the hole, Dio was dying of thirst. More than anything, he was dying inside. He felt dead. At the very least, he felt like he wanted to be dead. His baby had left him. His baby had left him alone and he felt empty inside. He felt the kind of hurt you feel when you can't feel anymore. He felt numb.

He couldn't fathom living without Jennifer.

She was probably just being manipulated by her family. That had to be it. They probably forced her to break up with him, or got her when she was low and not completely herself and fed thoughts inside her head.

His pride said, "Just fuck her. You can pick up some other bitch." But the truth was that he didn't want anybody else. Only she completed him, like no other. Living without her was like living without a piece of his soul; it was inconceivable.

He felt stupid for falling for Groissaint's trap. He should have seen it coming. Dio considered himself very streetwise, but he must have been blinded by his thoughts of Jennifer. All he knew was Groissaint was going to regret what he did to him.

He may not get it right away, but he's going to get it, Dio thought.

After all, "They hit you; you gotta hit 'em worse," Spooky used to always say. And he was right.

—

"For Christ's sakes!" Louise blurted out.

She wore the pants in the boot camp kitchen. If anyone ran the place, she did, and the last thing she wanted was another trainee to baby-sit. She shook her head at Dio as she rested her hands on her hips. She looked like she had just walked away from working at Wal-Mart or something. Not that anything was wrong with that. After all, Dio's mom had worked at Wal-Mart for a while. But it was true though, she was scary: trailer-trash-looking, stringy, badly permed hair, no makeup, a pruned-up, wrinkled face, and hardly any front teeth.

"I can't believe this," she added. "God dammit. If it's not

one thing, it's another. Well, I guess we better find you something to do."

She threw up her hands and led Dio out of the mess hall and into the back of the kitchen. There were already a bunch of workers cleaning every which corner, busier than bees.

"I keep telling that man I got shit to do, and he keeps sending me more."

She led Dio to a mountain of dishes bigger than Dio had ever seen before.

"Well, get at it," she demanded. "Lunch prep will be coming in an hour and you gotta get it all done by then."

Dio sighed. On one hand, he was just glad to be out of the hole. On the other hand, the last thing he wanted to do was more work—not this kind of work, of all things. He'd promised himself he'd never turn out like his father. His father was a janitor for years before he died. He'd come home drenched in dirty water, smelling like shit, and Dio was ashamed of him. He was a smart man, a very smart man at that, and a good father, but Dio hated seeing someone like him cleaning up after people. *Other kids in school had dads who were lawyers and doctors and executives and things. Why'd mine have to be a janitor?*

There had to be an easier way; Dio knew it. His mom was no different. No matter how bad his mother treated him when he was little, no matter how drunk she'd been most of the time, he hated to see her suffer. He hated to see her work two or three jobs just to keep him and his little brother alive. And it was all for nothing anyway, because taxes would take half of it, and what was left hardly went to food at all—it went to bills and shit. She refused to get on welfare and refused to accept food stamps.

Her mother, his grandmother, "came to this country to raise responsible members of society," she'd say, "not freeloaders."

Dio didn't see such a big deal with accepting food stamps or welfare. He figured the government screwed most people anyway, and besides, *what's the harm in getting a little help when you needed it?*

He hated seeing his mother come home exhausted, only to find an empty refrigerator and his little brother, Daniel, crying because he was hungry. No wonder she'd rather be in a drunken stupor. That's what led Dio to do what he liked to call "alternative means of income." What was the big deal about selling a little dope, if it was going to keep his mom from one more job? Besides, he was only "providing for the community," Dio would often joke.

And now here he was washing dish after nasty, funky dish for a bunch of inmates. Just the thought of cleaning up after other people pissed Dio off.

"You've got to be kidding. Give me that," Louise demanded as she snatched a dish from Dio and showed him the "proper" way to wash it. "I don't have time for this. You're going to have to figure this out. Soak them thoroughly first, then soap them up, all right? Jeez."

And she was off to put out some other fire in the kitchen.

Whatever, bitch, Dio thought.

He wanted to just forget the whole thing, but he knew

the junior officers keeping watch over him wouldn't be having any of that. Besides, Dio also had the feeling someone like Louise could pretty much hold her own when it came to the trainees. She was the queen bee, the head honcho when it came to the kitchen, and no one questioned her.

Part of Dio kind of liked that. He had always liked strong women, hated seeing weak women who couldn't stand up for themselves. His mother was like that. Sure, she was strong when it came to him and his brother, but whenever some man came into her life, which was often, she'd turn into complete mush. There was always some loser she'd bring into the house, claiming, "He could be your daddy one day." He'd only end up picking on Dio or, worse yet, his little brother. Then Dio would have to kick his ass.

Dio sighed and wiped the steam from his sweaty brow. He noticed Simon staring at him in the distance, his mouth wide open like he was trying to catch flies or something. The minute he noticed Dio noticing him, he went back to sweeping the floors. Simon was always assigned to sweep the floors and take out the trash. The broom looked bigger than Simon was, like an ant carrying a hunk of bread.

"Whatchew want, foo'?" Dio asked.

Simon just kept working.

"Yeah, you just keep sweepin' there. Keep sweepin'," Dio said.

Dio watched him out of the corner of his eye. He felt sorry for him actually. He was a total loser. The sad thing was, Dio felt that, next to him, he was probably the loneliest kid on the planet.

I shouldn't have been that rude to him, Dio thought.

But he hated people staring. Besides, he didn't want someone like that trying to be friends with him. If he was ever going to get respect from the other trainees, he was going to need someone who could match up to him, and Simon, well . . . just wasn't it.

He could hear Jennifer's voice now: "That's mean!" God, he missed her. Dio knew that she hadn't just told him to "fuck off." She did say they still had a connection. That had to mean there was hope to win her back. She just wanted him to "get help," to "straighten his life out." That had to mean that she did want them to be back together, didn't it?

Dio knew that he hadn't been the best boyfriend in the world. She had begged him over and over again to get out of the gang. She didn't seem to understand—once a gangsta, always a gangsta. He was branded for life. But deep inside, Dio knew she was right. Living the life he was leading was not the way to go. It really wasn't the way he wanted to go. He wanted so much more. He wanted the things he saw on TV, living the life that people on there had. He wanted to see the world and take Jennifer to exotic places. He wanted them to raise a family.

He'd dropped out of school when he was in the seventh grade, and though his mother screamed at him and berated him every day for doing it, what was he supposed to do? Why be somewhere where the teachers obviously didn't want him? They treated him like a second-class citizen, worse than that, actually. They'd make racist remarks and then wonder why he'd get pissed off. It wasn't like he didn't try to catch up in the overcrowded class, but he was embarrassed to ask questions because the teachers always had a way of making him feel stupid for asking them. And really they'd do worse that that. They'd make the whole class know just how stupid his question was.

It was much more fun hanging with his homies during school hours anyway. At least they accepted him for what he was. At least he didn't have to explain himself or why he was out of class. They knew why. They'd all had the same experiences. White people hated them and they hated white people in return.

Dio wiped the sweat off his brow again as he finished the last dish. He sighed with relief.

"Did I say you could take a break?" Louise asked, piling up an even bigger load of dishes in front of him.

Inmates brought in carton after carton of more dishes for him to wash. It was going to be a long day.

Dio could think of nothing better than getting to his bed and lying down after all that work. Not only was he exhausted from working in the kitchen all day, but he still had to do all the ridiculous calisthenics Jackson made them do. But a surge of energy ran through Dio at the sight of Grossaint. He was taking off his shirt when Dio noticed for the first time the swastika on his tricep.

They spotted each other at the same time and it was as if

the seas parted. Dio made his way over to him. They just glared at each other, nose to nose for a moment, both anticipating a move, but knowing they couldn't make one. Grossaint had the strangest wavering eyes that never stood still. It was the first time Dio discovered Grossaint might be a little off . . .

Dio's hands were itching to break Grossaint's nose.

"Who you think you are, *ése?*"

Grossaint cracked a smile, gesturing to his cronies, who surrounded Dio and seemed to come out of thin air.

"Whatcha think you're going to do, huh? Stupid wetback."

The hair raised on the back of Dio's neck, always did when his temper flared. His nose flared. His eyes squinted.

"Whatchew want me to do, *puto?*"

"*Puto?* Is that some kind of stupid Mexican word or something? Like taco or burrito?"

His cronies laughed.

Dio stepped up even closer to him and spoke so only Grossaint could hear him. "I will get you," he threatened. "Maybe not now, maybe not tomorrow, but it's coming. It's coming."

Dio swore he saw a flinch of fear in Grossaint's eyes for a second, and that's all he needed to see. He knew Grossaint was nothing without his peckerwood friends, nothing at all, but unfortunately there were hardly any Chicanos in the squad, and Grossaint had a big enough crew to easily take him.

"You don't want to mess with me, spic."

The white boys closed their gap and moved in on Dio.

Then, like a hot knife through butter, a voice came, "Leave him alone!"

Everyone looked around to find the source of the sound. Grossaint snickered when he saw who it was. It was Simon. He looked like a little boy who knew he had a whipping coming.

"Don't bother him."

Dio was shocked. This scrawny little thing was coming to his defense? *What did he think he was going to do? Slap them to death?*

"Shut up, stupid nigger," Grossaint answered. His boys laughed.

Something burned in Simon's eyes, a rage. A rage that was inside, but too afraid to come out.

"You shut up," he answered back and shrank back like he was a turtle crawling into his shell.

Grossaint seemed to be a lot more entertained by him than by Dio at the moment.

"Dumb coons just don't know when to keep their mouth shut."

He took a step toward Simon, but Dio stepped in his path. Grossaint was about to say something when someone yelled, "Officer on deck!"

Everyone scurried to their bunks and stood at the foot of them, standing erect as Jackson marched inside. He sensed something was off and immediately went to what had to be source of the trouble.

"What's going on in here? Radigez?"

"Sir, nothing, sir," Dio answered back.

Jackson looked him in the eyes as if he were trying to see right through him. He paced down the aisle to ask another trainee, "That true?"

"Sir, yes, sir," he answered.

Swift as a sword he turned to Simon. "That true?"

Simon swallowed hard. He never was any good at lying. "Uh—"

"Sir, you got a phone call," a junior officer called out.

Saved by the bell.

He exited, looking at everyone suspiciously. They all sighed with relief when he left.

Dio lay in bed and glanced at Groissant, who slid his finger across his throat at him. Dio flipped him the finger and caught a look at Simon, who seemed lost in his own world. He wanted to say thanks to him. It wasn't like he actually would have been able to do anything, but he admired Simon's courage. Maybe he wasn't so bad after all. There was a spark in Simon that Dio liked, a loyalty and courage that his best homies back home had.

They only had so many hours to sleep before they'd have to get up and start the whole day again, but Dio decided maybe he'd try to write Jennifer a letter. It was clear that he'd probably never get a chance to call her again, not after the last stunt he pulled. But there was some paper in his box with all the rest of his stuff, and a pencil. He just wanted to connect to her in some way and maybe that was it. What was the worst that could happen? He just hoped she'd get the letter. If her mom had anything to do with it, she never would.

Dear Jennifer,

Baby I am so sorry about what happened. You know that.
Don't you? You know I'd never wish anything like this to happen to
you. Everyday I wake up in the middle of the night and mi corazon
me duele, 'cause I know everything that's happened to you ~~ain't
right~~ is my fault.

I know you're enojada con migo. I know you have every right
to be mad but please don't let what other people say make you
not want to be with me. They don't know me like you know me.
You know what kind of person I am inside. What happens to you
and me is our business. It ~~got~~ has nothing to do with them. Te
amo, you know that. You know I don't want nothing to happen
to you.

If I could do it all over again I would but I can't. Please forgive me, please you can't leave me like this. Te necesito. Eres mi
vida. All I think about day and night is you. You don't know what
it's like. They got me stretched out.

For almost a month nobody told me if you were dead or
alive and I was depressed and I was tearing up inside cause
nobody would let me use the phone or nothing. No one would
tell me if you was alive or dead or anything. You ~~just have to~~
gotta believe me.

When I heard your voice on that phone you ~~had~~ have no idea
what that did to me. To hear that you were alive still. Baby I've
been dying inside every night thinking about you.

They don't let you do nothing here in camp Jennifer. Ni puedes
zurrar without asking permission. They don't let you talk, they
don't let you sit down, they don't let you eat, es como la pinta.
Nah, it's worse than prison. And all they do is talk masa in your

face all day. They don't care about you. They treat you like you're
a piece of *mierda*.

Baby you gotta know you're my everything y si te vallas. There'll
be nothing for me to live for. You can't just throw away all that we've
been through together. ~~We've been through so much and~~ We've got a
future together I know it.

Don't give up on me. You're the only one I got left beside my
hermanito. And my moms is filling Daniel's head up with a bunch
of masa about me too. Nobody cares about me like you care about
me. Just the thought of losing you completely destroys me.

You taught me so much and I'm going to change I promise.
I'm trying my best when I get out things are going to be so much
better. Te lo prometo. You'll see. Just give me another chance, I'll
prove it to you. ~~Please baby, I need you.~~

Write me back as soon as you can. There's no one to chop it
up with here at all. You should hear the shit these babosos call me.
I gotta keep trucha when I'm around these putos. I know they're
just waiting for their chance to catch me slippin'. I'm trying to be
good cause I want to get out of here as fast as I can so I can be
with you ~~again~~. But sometimes I feel like takin' a filero to these
peckerwoods throats, but I'm being good for you baby, I'm going
to change for you.

Estoy aquí para ti. No matter what, siempre. Remember?

Love,
Playboy

The whole next day Jackson had them digging ditches. Why?
Because Jackson said it built *indefatigability*.

"Do you know what *indefatigability* is, Trainee Radigez?"
he asked.

"Sir, no, sir," Dio answered.

Jackson sighed and shook his head. "Take a wild guess."

"Sir, muscles, sir?" Dio answered.

"No, no, and no!" Jackson responded. "*Indefatigability*
is being seemingly incapable of being fatigued. You build
stamina; you don't get so tired so easily."

Well whoop-dee-do, who cares? Dio thought.

It seemed Jackson loved to make them work like horses.
He said it was to build indefatigability, but Dio figured it
was probably just to piss them off. And he had thought the
dishes and scrubbing the floor all day with a toothbrush
was bad. Digging ditches had to be the hardest work he had
ever done.

Jackson pushed and pushed them, going on and on, saying things like, "How you like that, huh? You like digging
them ditches? You like it? Move!" He'd taunt them and somehow it was supposed to encourage them to move faster? It
only pissed them off more.

"You wanna spend the rest of your life digging ditches,
just keep doing what you're doing in your life and the shovel
will be waiting for you."

Yeah, that's what Dio wanted to do for the rest of his
life, sure. With any luck he was going to get the hell out of
camp and get a legitimate job doing something that would
make Jennifer proud to be with him. He thought about going to work for a car design shop. He even thought about

going to night school or something and getting his diploma—whatever it took to win her back.

Dio wiped his brow in the hot sun. It was winter in the desert, but during the day it was just as hot as any time of the year. They had to be at least forty miles outside of Las Vegas and there was absolutely nothing around but the camp and the prison down the road. Dio daydreamed about escaping. It'd be so easy if it was night and somehow he got out and . . . but he put it out of his mind. If they ever caught anyone trying to escape, they'd be sent straight to prison for real, not three days in the hole. They'd be put in there for the full sentence.

Dio had been in and out of juvie since he was a kid, but that was preschool compared with what went down in the real prisons. Spooky would tell him stories of the brutality, the rapes, and the corruption that went on, not just with the prisoners, but also with the guards supervising the whole thing. That's how Spooky lost one of his eyes. He wasn't about to let some *puto* rape him.

Dio looked over his shoulder to see Simon struggling beside him. He took another whiff of his asthma inhaler and kept going.

"Hey," Dio called, careful that nobody but Simon could hear him.

"We're not supposed to be talking," Simon answered.

Dio smacked his lips. "That foo's not going to do nothing to me he ain't done already."

Simon's eyes lit up a bit.

"I 'preciate you sticking up for me last night. It was coo'," Dio said. "It was stupid, but it was coo'."

A smile spread across Simon's face. "Thanks!"

"Sssh," Dio cautioned. "Keep it on the down-low."

"On the down-low?" Simon asked. He sounded like a fucking white boy. He had no clue what Dio was saying.

"Yeah, you know. Keep the volume down, foo', you black and you don't know what that means?"

Simon looked like a shamed boy.

"I'm not all the way black," he answered.

"What are you?"

"My dad's black, my mom's Hispanic."

"For real? That almost makes us brothers."

"It does?" Simon asked with a smile.

"Sure, and us brownskins gotta stick together, right? That's why you gotta help me get back at Grossaint somehow."

Dio tried to give him daps, his fist ready to connect with Simon's, but Simon didn't have a clue what he was doing.

"Don't leave me hangin', nigga," Dio said, grabbing Simon's scrawny little fist and showing him what to do.

Simon smiled sheepishly.

Dio shook his head. "Whatchew in here for anyway? You're too skinny to be in a gang, too prude to hotwire a car."

Simon withdrew. Whatever it was he'd done, he was too ashamed to even talk about it.

"Come on, foo', you can tell me. I got in here for possession of a firearm. Wrong place, wrong time. Lucky for the *putos* we were about to hit that we got caught, 'cause they'd be dead by now."

"You were going to shoot them?"

"'Course. They tried to kill me in a drive-by. Got my girl instead."

Dio tried to get the thought out of his head. He'd been plagued by nightmares the last couple of nights. He kept seeing those two punks who had shot Jennifer, Acne and Dirty Blond, laughing at him over and over again. "Don't fuck with me, spic," they kept saying.

"Is she dead?"

"Nah. Thank God for that. She laid up in the hospital, but she'll get better. And when I get out, me and my *jaina* going to hook up like nobody's business."

"*Jaina?*"

"Yeah, you know, *mi ruca, mi jaina,* my girl, my lady."

"Oh."

"*Simón, ése.*"

"*Simón?* I don't speak Spanish."

Dio shook his head. "*Órale. Simón.* You know. That's like saying, 'That's live. That's money.'"

Simon still looked confused as hell. Dio thought for a second.

"You know, 'That's cool, dude.'"

The lightbulb came on in Simon's head and he smiled, nodding like a bobble-head toy.

Dio was surprised at how open he was with Simon. Normally he clammed up with strangers, but there was something so nonthreatening about Simon, so innocent, it was refreshing. Besides, who else was he going to talk to? Though he hated to admit it, Simon was the closest thing to a homie he had in the whole place.

"*Órale. Simón,*" Simon repeated to himself like he'd just discovered the secrets of the universe.

Later that day, Jackson had some brainiac idea about a trust exercise. He had all the guys pair up into couples, which he randomly selected, and had them fall backward. The other one was supposed to catch them. It was supposed to teach them trust or something like that . . . so he said.

Dio knew it was an accident waiting to happen. Nobody trusted anyone there. Most of them had lived on the wrong side of the tracks just like he did. They were naturally cautious. They slept with one eye open just like him. They never let anyone get real close because they knew at any moment their so-called "boy" could and probably would stab them right in the back.

Luckily, Dio got paired up with some crony of Grossaint's who "accidentally" almost dropped him. Dio knew not to trust him, so he was prepared to catch himself. Dio made sure to whisper something in his ear to make sure he never tried to pull that stunt again. Whatever it was, he turned pale afterward and couldn't wait to get away from him.

Dio looked a few hundred feet away at an older squad of guys wearing all white, who snickered as they watched Dio and his squad. They were in the last level and obviously ready to graduate. The guys glared at them.

"What the hell you looking at?" Jackson asked. "You think you'll ever get there? Half you guys won't even make it past this level, 'specially since you can't get the molasses out of your asses and the cotton from your brains to think!"

And just like that, just as Dio had predicted might happen, Simon fell right on his ass. Of course, everyone laughed except for Dio and Jackson. *Didn't Jackson ever have a sense of humor about nothing?*

"Boy, what in the hell is wrong with you?" he asked Simon. "Can't you stand up straight?"

"Sir, yes, sir. It's just that Trainee, that guy—"

"That guy, this guy, I don't want to hear any excuses. There are no excuses in life, Simon. You point at someone and you're pointing three fingers back at yourself. Now get back in line," Jackson demanded.

He turned to Groissant and quick as a flash said, "Catch me." He let himself fall right into Grossaint's arms. Luckily Grossaint was quick on his feet. Dio would have loved to see Jackson fall right on his ass.

"Trust is a very important thing. If you can't trust nobody, then you can't trust yourself. And for all you idiots out there that think it's funny to drop each other, just know karma—what goes around comes around. Ya hear?"

That didn't make any sense as far as Dio was concerned. It seemed like any time Dio tried to do something nice for someone, it always backfired. It was like, "no good deed goes unpunished," just like Spooky used to tell him.

All of a sudden a shitty-looking mutt came from the main building and ran toward them. Simon ducked like it was about to attack him or something, but it ran right to Jackson's side, and he smiled.

"Good girl. This is Coffee and she's probably about the closest thing to pussy you're going to get while you're here, so treat her right. You'll see her making her way around here just like anybody else and it will be your responsibility to care for her. That means feeding her, cleaning up after her, keeping her out of trouble. Shit, you hardly can keep yourself out of trouble, but . . . she's here to stay."

Most of the guys had a twinkle in their eyes at the sight of the dog. She was about the ugliest thing Dio had ever seen, but she seemed friendly and came right up to most of the guys. He petted her. She wasn't as nice as the Rottweiler he had back at home when he was a kid, but she'd have to do. They called his Rott Buddy. He had to be the most loyal dog there ever was. His mom named him. Dio never would have given him some name like that. He practically surgically attached himself to Jennifer. It was always a friendly competition for attention between Dio and Buddy.

"Anyway, you keep your nose clean the next couple of weeks, eat all your peas and carrots, and you'll make it to Visitor's Day."

Excitement ran through the whole troop. Wow! Visitor's Day. Dio was buzzing inside. He'd invite Jennifer to come. God, he needed to see her. Maybe she could get someone to take her out there, probably not her parents, but maybe some friend of hers. That was the first good news Dio had heard since he got to camp.

Then again, he still hadn't heard back from her yet. It had only been two days since he sent the letter, but he knew it would take at least a couple of days for her to respond. He kept thinking that she was probably reading the letter now, and that thought kept him feeling warm inside. He could see her now, lying in her hospital bed, her long, flowing hair on her shoulders. He could see it all now, with her opening his letter and smelling it for his scent. She was alone, nobody to distract her or to feed her bad thoughts about him—just him and her. They were connected; he knew it. They always had been; they always would be.

Jackson always had some new idea he would come up with. Dio hadn't a clue where he found them, probably an old episode of *Dr. Phil* or *Oprah* or something. This time around he figured he'd make it a rule that any time somebody had a birthday, everyone in the squad was responsible for making some kind of birthday gift for them. It could be a home-made card, some kind of craft thing they'd cut and glued together, or something from their personal possessions. Since most of them hadn't anything to call their own, most of them ended up making something from scratch.

First up, it was Grossaint's birthday. It was almost St. Patrick's Day. Dio would much rather have spent the weekend with Jennifer, drinking green beer at Spooky's or something. Grossaint kept bragging that he was part Irish, so Dio thought he'd give him something to remember his heritage by, something that he'd remember for a long time.

For some strange reason, Coffee had taken a liking to Grossaint. She seriously would not leave his side, no matter how many times he pushed her away. He'd threaten her, he'd pull her by the tail, but no matter what, she was completely in love with him. He tried to get rid of her time and time again, but Dio thought that he secretly liked all the attention. Just like he liked the attention he was getting from most of the guys. He had naturally decided he'd pretty much be the leader for the whole squad and just about everyone accepted it— other than Dio and Simon, of course.

Every day that week Jackson made them race in a sort of obstacle course, with things to jump over, walls to scale, and ropes to climb. Grossaint always won. Jackson timed them all in a race. Dio didn't even try. Why bother? He hated all that shit and he was just going to lose anyway. Grossaint always had some smart-ass comment to make when Dio came in last, like, "Come on, Mexican jumping bean." And he'd always time it perfectly, so he could say it and get away with it just as Jackson was stepping away.

Dio approached Grossaint as he ripped open his birthday presents like a spoiled-rotten brat. He was loving every moment of it, though he didn't like to show it. Dio could see right through him. His ice-blue eyes looked up at Dio suspiciously as Dio handed him a handmade card. He took it like he was about to open a bomb and pried it open carefully. Seeing there was nothing in it, he read it. It had a simple picture of a flower and "Happy Birthday. Good luck in the races."

Seeing there was nothing more to it than that, Grossaint crumpled it in his hand, tossed it away, and began to open the other presents.

"Chow time!" a junior officer yelled.

Everyone got up, put their shoes on, and headed out. When Grossaint did the same, he was shocked at the gooshing sensation from his shoes. Then he sat back down and pulled his shoes off, only to sniff the funky smell of dog shit all over his feet.

"Oh, shit!" Grossaint exclaimed.

Dio and Simon hid around the corner, trying not to laugh too hard. Grossaint looked everywhere for them. He knew who was behind it.

Dio and Simon were walking swiftly by him when Simon turned around and said, "Happy Birthday," and laughed. Dio nudged him.

"Stupid. Keep it on the down-low." He turned to see Grossaint's teeth grit, his face beet red with anger. He shook his head in a deathly threat.

Dio knew he was in for it, in for something big this time. It was no longer fun and games. It was war.

Chapter Three

HE COULDN'T OPEN THE ENVELOPE QUICKLY ENOUGH. IT had been two weeks since he had sent Jennifer the letter and finally she had written him back. Tearing open the letter was like tearing off Jennifer's clothes.

He wanted to read it as soon as he got it, but it was kitchen-duty time and he knew what would happen if he were late. He was supposed to be cleaning out the grease traps, but he stole away a few minutes in the corner to read it.

Dear Dio,

It took me a long time to write this letter cause I'm in such pain. The medicine that they put me on makes me feel sick to my stomach. You don't know what it's been like for me laying up in the hospital like this. You say you're sorry, you say you care for me, pero no te creo. I think all you think about is yourself.

I think you're completely selfish. I sacrificed a lot for you. I've made enemies out of my friends and out of my family when all along all they were doing was just trying to save me from you. They were right, I always knew it inside. I knew you were no good for me. I knew you were trouble, you've always been trouble. I've tried to save you so many times. You don't know what it's like for me to constantly have to defend you to all my friends.

It's hard for me to see you like this Dio, when I know you can be so much more. But you keep messing things up. It's like you say you want to change and you know you can be better but you're afraid of it at the same time. No te entiendo. It doesn't make any sense.

It's so painful for me. They say I almost died Dio. They say one of the bullets was just centimeters from my corazon. I should have been dead but somebody's watching over me and I can only think it's because I'm supposed to be here for some reason. It's like a second chance and I've got to do things right this time.

I want to believe you Dio. I want to believe that this time it will be different that you will change but I just don't see how. I don't know how that's possible. Everything you've said you'd do you haven't done. You said you'd get a regular job, but you ended up selling drugs. You said you'd get out of all that gang banging shit but instead you kicked it with your cholo friends all the time. Quit trying to save them all the time, they don't need your help. You need your help. I need your help. What about me? Is your love for them more important than me?

Friends will come and go Dio, but true love lasts forever. Nunca te olvidas de eso. I feel torn too Dio. I want to believe it that you'll turn things around I just don't know if it's true. I want to believe it's true but I don't know Dio. You've got to show me. When I see you in a shirt and tie and you've got a real job and *you've been holding it down for long time and you've got a place of your own and you're not talking like a thug anymore then maybe I'll believe it. You've got so much potential Dio. I just wish you'd focus on that and forget all that other crap.*

You know what I think Dio. I think it's karma. I think you've walked through most of life without really getting your just due, you knew your mama would just bail you out. Well I think life caught up to you and I think life's teaching you a lesson. You do the crime you've got to do the time. It's true.

My whole family hates you now. If they even knew I was writing back to you they'd go crazy. I had to sneak this letter out to you through the nurse. My familia would never understand. Just get better okay? Do something with your life and use this time in camp to really think about things.

Jennifer

The letter tore Dio apart. Part of him was just glad that she had written him back, but it wasn't what he wanted to hear. He wanted so badly for her to just forgive him. He knew that what had happened was serious, but to hear her say things like that, it was like losing his best friend all over again. He couldn't bear the thought of it.

He read it over and over again just to see if he'd gotten it right, but it was the same each time. The letter never changed. Dio closed his eyes. He felt like he was sinking inside. Maybe he should just accept the fact that—

"Oh, for heaven's sake!" It was Louise, yelling about something in the other room.

Dio shook his head and started cleaning the grease traps again. But then he thought he heard a sniffle.

Could it be?

It almost sounded as if Louise was . . . he had to check it out. He wiped his hands off and moved toward the source of the sound.

Louise was in the pantry and she had her back turned. Her arms were folded and she seemed to be having trouble stocking the canned goods.

Dio cleared his throat. "You all right?"

"Jeez!" she exclaimed. "Scared the shit out of me."

"Well, sorry, I was just—" He stopped. Her face was red, her eyes still soaked. It was clear that she had just been crying, no matter how quickly she tried to wipe her tears.

"What do you want?" she snapped.

"You all right?"

"Yeah, 'course I am. You just mind your own goddamn business and get back to work."

"Whatever," Dio muttered, and turned to leave.

He was just trying to help.

Why'd she have to be such a bitch about it?

But then he stopped and listened. She started crying again.

God, he hated to see a woman cry. It brought him back to seeing his mother lying in bed for weeks at a time because some asshole she thought was her boyfriend had just swept her aside like yesterday's trash. He hated it when she brought over their "new daddy" because he could always read people and he just knew they were going to end up hurting her. At first, he would tell her how much he didn't like them, that they gave him a bad vibe, but she'd just shoo him off and say he didn't know what he was talking about. He wouldn't dare say, "I told you so." That would be disrespectful. But he knew it and she knew it and nothing more needed to be said.

A woman crying made him feel powerless, like a train wreck was about to happen and there was nothing he could do about it. Maybe she just wanted to be left alone.

Then he thought of something, something that always made his mother and Jennifer happy whenever they were down. There wasn't much to choose from, but he went outside and looked around for whatever he could find until he found it.

He came into the pantry, approaching her with caution as she sobbed in the corner, and left a flower he had picked. It wasn't much, just a violet he had found outside. Some people would consider it a weed, but that's all he knew to do. He had started to go out of the pantry room when . . .

"Hey. Get over here," Louise said.

Dio obeyed.

"Yeah?" he answered.

"What was that for?"

Dio shrugged. "I don't know."

"You picked that outside for me?"

"It's no big deal," Dio said, turning to leave.

"Wait a minute. I didn't say you could go. Get your ass over here."

"What?" Dio asked.

"You trying to be sweet to me or something? Whatcha up to, huh? Whatcha want?"

"Nothing. I don't want nothing. Just thought you could use something to lift your spirits."

"That it, huh?"

"Yep."

She grunted. "Well, don't think you gonna get anything out of it or nothing."

"Whatever."

She was hardheaded. He could see that right away. It was probably just as hard for her to say "Thank you" or "I'm sorry" or any of the other things that made you feel weak, but were so important to say, as it was for him. He felt for her. She didn't have to say any of those things that he knew she was saying inside.

"I'm not trying to get up in your business or nothing, but what was the matter anyway?" he asked.

"Don't ever get married. That's what's the matter," she snapped back.

"Relationship shit? I know how that goes."

"Yeah? What do you know about relationships?"

"I got female problems, that's what."

"What kind of female problems?"

"Got a girl. She mad at me right now."

"She got a reason?"

Dio thought awhile. "Kinda."

"What is it?"

"She got a reason. That's all," he answered. "Why do females got to be so complicated? I tried to say I'm sorry.

I wrote her a letter and everything, but girls want you down on your knees. They want to drag shit out and make you feel as low as you can."

"Is that so?"

"Yeah, that's so. Didn't used to be like this. Wish it could be like it used to."

He was lost in the thought. Louise started putting things away in the pantry again.

"Well, that's the way it goes. Relationships fade," she said.

"Not me and Jennifer. We're soul mates. We're . . . we're . . ."

"Connected?"

"Yeah. Exactly. Connected like nobody's business. I look at her and I know we're going to be together forever. We just going through a little bit of a bump."

Dio took the letter out of his pocket. "I know I'm not supposed to bring this to work, but . . . she said it right here: 'It's karma.' She don't want nothing to do with me. She don't know how much I love her."

"Well, if you don't believe in yourself, how do you expect her to? She wrote you back? What'd she say?"

"You ain't going to squeal on me or nothing for bringing this, are you?"

"Just read the damn letter."

Dio read the letter to her. She just listened and thought in silence for a long time. Finally Dio couldn't take it anymore. Patience never had been his best quality.

"Well?" he insisted.

"Sounds like she still wants you."

"For real?"

She looked in his eyes. She could see right through him, right to his heart. He really loved this girl.

"Yeah, listen to what she's saying. Give me that," she said, snatching the letter from him. "Listen, 'Friends will come and go but true love lasts forever . . . when I see you in a shirt and tie and you've got a real job . . .' She's telling you she wants you back. Just get your shit together."

"For real?"

"For real? Of course, for real. What's that supposed to mean? You're talking to a woman here. And I've got two teenage daughters that give me hell. I know these things. Besides, if she was really over you, she never would have written you back."

Then she looked at him softly, probably more softly than he'd even seen her, and said, "I'm Louise."

"Dio."

"I know who you are. Listen, if what you're saying is true and you really are soul mates, Dio, don't let her get away. Write her back. You still got a chance with her."

Dio felt all sorts of exuberance inside, and a newfound hope. He was anxious. She was right; she had to be. She was a woman and she knew what women wanted.

"What should I say? What should I say?"

Dio thought long and hard about everything Louise said to him that day. Most of it made a lot of sense. She told him to speak from the heart. She said the problem with men is that they feel all these things inside, but they never communicate them to their women. Their women feel neglected and insecure.

"It's all about communication," she said.

He drew a beautiful picture of Jennifer, tracing every detail of her angelic face in his mind, thinking over and over again about what he wanted to say. He sat up on his hard-as-wood bunk and began to write.

Dear Jennifer,

Why you have to make me feel like shit? You know I mean every ~~thing~~ word I say to you girl. You know that everything I say is from my heart. Todo. And I'm going to prove it to you. When I get out I'm going to be a completely different man. You'll see.

You mean so much to me. You mean the world to me and you know this baby.

You know sometimes the things I mean in my head ~~sometimes they~~ don't exactly come out the way they're supposed to. You've got to just know what's in my corazon. I've always been there for you. Tu saves eso. You know if I was there right now I'd be laying in bed with you, ~~lying next to you,~~ holding you. I'd be stroking your pelo, kissing your labios, making you feel good. You know that's all I think about here, being with you. It's the only thing that gets me through the day.

This place is like hell. Most the day I think I'm goin loco. It's not just all the hard work they make us do. Chingan con tu mente.

They even got some of the hardest vatos in here in tears cause of the shit they say. It's like psychology shit ~~or something~~ and they're always screaming at you, just like my moms used to do me. It's like living with my moms all over again. Me estan acabando.

I don't want you to think I'm acting like a chavala, Jennifer cause you know that ain't me but I just want to let you know I'm not having an easy time with this, tampoco. I don't know how much more of this I can take and I don't know how I'm going to make it through a whole year like this. The only thing I have to look forward to is ~~when~~ that I might get a letter back from you.

The mail only comes una vez a la semana, and my heart pounds every time they pass it out cause I'm hoping I'll get something from you.

That's what you do to me baby, you make my heart pound, and you make me feel vivo. I know you're going to pull through in the hospital and I'm going to get out and we're going to be together and things are going to be ~~better~~ much better. You'll see.

Every night I fall asleep thinking about you. I think about you as soon as I wake up. I think about you in the day when they have us doing all this exercise shit.

Baby like I said, sometimes it's not easy for me to get what's in me out so I hope you can just feel what I'm trying to say. Just know that in your heart, whatever you need to hear, whatever it would take to make you feel better I'm there for you.

I almost forgot Visitor's Day is coming up next Friday at 6pm. You think you can

"Wow, you drew that? That's beautiful. Whatcha doing?" Simon asked.

"You messin' my vibe, man," Dio answered.

Simon backed away like he just had been slapped across the face, which only made Dio feel bad.

"I'm just writing Jennifer."

"Your *jaina*."

Dio smiled. "*Simón*. I can't spell too good. How you spell *knot*?"

"Depends if you mean *not* like I cannot or *knot* as in a ship's directional course. And of course there's *naught* as in—"

"Okay, okay. I'm talking about like 'my stomach's in knots.'"

"Oh! K-n-o-t. Can I see your letter?" Simon peered over his shoulder to take a look. Dio slid out of the way.

"Man, you're nosy."

"Sorry."

Dio sighed. "Look, don't you got a girl of your own? Jeez."

"My parents won't let me."

"Won't let you? How old are you?"

"Just turned eighteen."

"And they won't let you?"

"It's against my religion."

"What religion is that?"

Simon shied away. "Just Christian."

"What kind of Christian religion don't let you date nobody?"

"I gotta wait 'til I'm thinking about marriage. I'm not ready yet. Besides, who would ever have me?"

"Dude, you need to get some balls. Get some confidence. You don't believe in you, how's somebody else supposed to?"

Dio couldn't believe he had just said that. It was like he was possessed by the spirit of Louise. But she did have a point.

"Yeah, I guess."

"Man, somebody got to teach you to strut. You can't just walk around like you're Eeyore all the time. How you expect anybody to respect you?"

"Yeah, listen to him. He'll teach you a thing or two," Grossaint blurted out, petting Coffee.

"Shut the fuck up, *ése*. Man, I ain't in the mood for you. Just go back to sleep," Dio said.

"What are you, Casanova or something?" Grossaint sneered.

"What?"

"You don't know who Casanova is? Dumb fuck."

Dio started for him, but Coffee got up and started growling at him.

Grossaint smiled at the dog, surprised. "Good dog."

Simon tugged at Dio. "It's not worth it," Simon said. "They'll just send you back in the hole. Think about your girl."

Dio hated to admit it, but Simon was right. No matter how much he wanted to just pound Grossaint right then and there, it would just cause more problems.

"You think you're so smart. You're in camp just like the rest of us."

"Yeah, but at least I'm going somewhere when I get out. You'll just be stuck in the ghetto."

"I ain't going to be in no ghetto. Soon as I get out I'm going to be a artist, a car design shop artist."

Grossaint laughed in his face. "You're dreaming. You're going right back to the ghetto."

Dio could have hit him at that moment. He was going to be somebody; he just knew it.

"Yeah? Well, at least I'm not going to go back to that trailer park with Ma and Pa and your girlfriend—I mean, your sister," Dio said.

The guys busted out laughing. It took Dio by surprise. It was the first sign of anything positive from the guys.

Dio started flapping his arms and slapping his thigh like he was some kind of country boy. "Get off me, brother. Get off me."

"You're just stupid. I got a girl at home and at least she ain't some slut like you probably got."

"Don't talk about my girl like that."

"Don't talk about my girl like that," Grossaint mimicked. He obviously was feeling joy at finding something that hurt Dio as well. "Y'all Mexicans breed like roaches. She's probably fat and pregnant with your baby, or some other dude's by now."

"Fuck you, man."

"She probably got some kind of gonorrhea or syphilis or something. Probably on welfare, or picking some strawberries in somebody's field."

Dio was burning up as Grossaint and his boys started cracking up, adding little comments here and there.

"She's just a dumb wetback, just like you," Grossaint added. If Simon hadn't tugged at Dio again to snap him out of the rage he was about to go into, he probably would have snapped Grossaint's neck.

"My girl got more smarts in her pinky than the whole lot of you got in all y'all's bodies. Least she ain't as dumb as your mama."

Grossaint froze. Blood rushed to his face.

"Lay off my mom."

"I tried, but I'm next in line."

Everyone cracked up.

"Least my mom ain't some Mexican jumping bean, probably spreading her legs for every—"

"That all you got to say? Yeah? Well, your mama so dumb if she could speak her mind, she'd be speechless."

The guys busted out laughing.

"Yo mama so dumb, the only job she could get was a blow job."

Grossaint was taken aback; even his cronies were trying not to laugh.

"Yo mama so dumb, wait . . . she had you."

"I told you. Don't talk about my mom like that."

Dio could see in his eyes that Grossaint was serious. He'd struck a chord, something deep inside Grossaint, though he couldn't put his finger on it. And something told him not to go there. Not now.

"Whatever, you lily-white peckerwood. You ain't worth my time anyway."

⌇

Dio was counting the days to Visitor's Day. Then counting the hours. He stayed up the whole night before thinking about seeing Jennifer again. He hadn't gotten a letter back from her yet, but then again, he figured she probably just planned to show up. It didn't make sense to write back.

The room was already packed with guests when the squad entered the room in a single-file line. When Jackson alerted the guys to go see their guests, they were like little kids again. Dio waited for Jennifer with the other guys who were waiting for their guests. And he waited and he waited until nobody was left in line except him and Simon.

"Where's your girl, Dio?"

"She's probably just running late or something. She'll be here. You'll see."

"Can't wait to see her."

"Yep. Where's your mom and dad?"

Simon shrugged.

"Fuck them."

"Yeah," Simon agreed.

"They just missing out."

Simon sniffled, "Yeah."

"Who needs them? They don't want to show up, you don't want them to show up."

Simon's eyes watered. He sniffled again. "Yeah . . . I gotta go to the bathroom."

Dio watched as he trailed off to ask Jackson for permission to use the head.

Poor kid, Dio thought.

Dio knew he was much stronger than Simon would ever be. He wondered what his whole story was. Simon didn't look tough enough to hurt a fly. Seemed like he had a heart of gold.

What parent wouldn't want him?

Dio waited by himself as guests came and went. Even Grossaint had a guest. Some big guy who looked like he was probably his brother. He had a wife-beater on and dirty blond hair, with the same ice-blue eyes that Grossaint had. He had tattoos up and down his arm like he had just come out of prison, too.

Dio watched Grossaint. He didn't put on the tough façade he did when was with the rest of the squad. He seemed like a little boy, excited about his brother or whoever the guy was.

He watched him as Grossaint's face turned from glee to completely pale as he listened to the guy. He looked like he was going to cry or something. Dio wondered what could be so awful that would turn his cold heart to mush. Whatever it was, it made Grossaint put his tough façade back on, lost in his thoughts as his brother straggled out of the visitors' room.

Dio waited and waited until there was no one left. He felt completely embarrassed as the squad one by one started lining up again. They looked at him with a "you-didn't-get-anybody-to-visit-you?" look that Dio hated. He just kept his chin up, looking straight ahead, though he was dying inside.

Jackson watched him from a distance. Then he came up to him and spoke in a low tone.

"Where's this lady friend of yours you were talking about?"

Dio was irritated.

He really knew how to rub something in.

"Sir, Trainee Rodríguez doesn't know, sir. Guess she couldn't make it, sir."

"Ah, I see. Well, there's always next time."

And he took off. Was that supposed to make him feel better or something? Dio just became more irritated, couldn't wait until he could hit the sack, get under his covers, and cry.

Must be some mistake, Dio thought. *She probably didn't get the letter or maybe she got the date mixed up. She wouldn't just dog me like that. Would she?*

⌁

"You're shitting me," Dio said, his eyes about to pop out.

He lay in his bunk and talked quietly to Simon. Everyone was talking very quietly. It was late at night and they knew they weren't supposed to, but no one seemed to be able to sleep.

"No, I'm serious. They own all of them," Simon responded nonchalantly.

"You're telling me every single Vegas Flower Express your family owns? You must be . . ."

"Millionaires?" Simon shrugged. "It's their money, not mine."

"So you grew up with like maids and butlers and stuff?"

"Something like that. It's not all it's cracked up to be."

"Man, if I had your family . . ."

"You can take them. Maybe they'd want you."

"Your family don't want you?"

Simon shrugged. He seemed uncomfortable with the question.

"Sure. I mean, when I'm not at my dad's, I'm at my mom's. Hardly see them though. Got so many stepbrothers and sisters. Only time they ever pay attention to me is when I need to . . . never mind."

He clammed up again. Every time Dio really started to get to know him, he'd do that. There was silence between them for a while. Dio looked over at that asshole Grossaint. He was chatting with his boys as usual. They always seemed to separate themselves from the rest of the squad, as if they were too good for them.

"That your brother that showed up last Visitor's Day?" Grossaint's skinny little sidekick Franklin asked.

"Yep," Grossaint answered, petting Coffee.

"He looks like you."

Grossaint smiled. "Yep, my big brother. He's got women lined up for miles. Got three right now."

"Three?"

"Yep."

"You got a girl?"

Grossaint seemed nervous. "'Course I do. Why? You fag. We . . . broke up right before I got in here."

"What was she like?"

"Pretty . . . blonde, brown eyes. Big tits."

"Sounds nice."

Grossaint shrugged. "Just like my dad used to say, 'You turn them all upside down and they're all sisters.'"

They roared with laughter. Dio knew if Jennifer heard Grossaint say something like that, she'd kick his ass.

"Where is your dad anyway?" Franklin asked.

"Don't know. It's been a while."

"How long?"

"Long enough. Went off the deep end. Thought I saw him once downtown on the streets. Tried to help him, but he was too drunk."

"Did he recognize you?"

"Thought he did, but who knows? I wanted us all to get together, the whole family for Christmas, just like old times, but . . . then I got locked up in here."

Grossaint sat up a little, excited. "Did you know you can call this 800 number and they can, like, find anybody on the planet? Anybody. Told my brother about it, might be able to find everyone once I get out."

"How many brothers and sisters you have?"

Grossaint smiled. "A lot. Nine of us."

"Damn! Can you name them all?"

"Of course. There's Joy, Michael, Travis, Steve, Joseph, um . . . um . . . Tracy, Terry . . . um . . ."

"You can't even remember them?"

"Shut the fuck up, can too! Johnny and Rachel, she's my twin."

"You're a twin?"

"Yep . . . haven't seen her, seen most of them, since . . . been years, except for Michael. That's the one that showed up last Visitor's Day." He lowered his voice, but Dio could still hear it. "You know, that's the problem with America today, too many Mexicans taking our jobs. We let too many illegals in, honest hard-working men losing their jobs, all 'cause of some fucking spics."

"Isn't that the truth?"

"Wrecking perfectly happy families."

Dio wondered if that's what happened to him. Maybe that was why he was so angry all the time. He blamed some Mexican guy for taking his dad's job.

But what did that have to do with him not seeing his family? Dio wondered.

~

Jennifer's not showing up for Visitor's Day just made Dio's weeks go on like hell. It had been three weeks since that day and Jennifer still hadn't written back. What was she trying to do, just forget him completely?

He just felt like he was going through the motions.

Why even try that hard? What good was it? What good was life at all without Jennifer?

Nothing was more obnoxious than those damn obstacle

courses. Jackson kept trying to time them all and they were supposed to be making some improvement each time. Dio didn't understand the whole point. He just wanted the day to get over with so he could get on with the next one, and the next and the next.

"Chow time," Jackson announced to the exhausted trainees. Excitement spread among them as they lined up for food.

Dio was starving to death and he couldn't wait to eat.

"Everyone get to it . . . except you, Radigez."

Dio froze.

Oh, shit, what is he doing now?

"Sir?" Dio said.

"You heard me. Get over here."

Dio tried to not show his disgust.

"Sir, yes, sir."

"What do you think you're doing today? My dead grandmother could do a better job."

"Sir, Trainee Rodríguez is just doing what you told him, sir."

"No, no, and no! What you're doing is a half-assed job. What I told you was to do them ropes and those walls as fast as you can."

"Sir—"

"You want some cheese with that whine of yours?"

"Sir, no, sir."

"What? What's your problem today? Need I remind you? The longer I don't see any improvement, the longer your sentence will be."

Dio sighed and muttered under his breath, as Jackson looked the other way.

"What?" Jackson asked, charging into Dio's face. "What'd you say? Speak up, boy. Stand up straight."

Dio straightened. "Sir, Trainee Rodríguez was just saying . . . he's doing his best, sir."

"Your best? Your best! I know best and that ain't it. What's wrong with you? You want to ever see that girl of yours again or what?"

"Sir, 'course I . . . Trainee Rodríguez does, sir."

"Hit dirt and give me one hundred."

"Sir?"

"Hit dirt and give me two hundred, then!"

Dio obeyed and started pounding out the pushups one at a time. Jackson kept him going like that for a half an hour; pushups, then sit-ups, then squats, anything he could think of. Every vein in Dio's neck was strained. His muscles were beyond sore. There was a pain that simply went beyond pain and Dio had it.

"You keep talking about this girl you want to see. You think she wants some half-assed man, some scum on the streets, some bum that can't get a job, some ignoramus that's going to be in and out of jail, some quitter?"

"Sir, no, sir."

"Give me a hundred more pushups."

"Sir, I . . . sir, Trainee Rodríguez can't, sir."

"Ninety percent mental, ten percent physical. There are no excuses in life, Radigez. *Can't* ain't a word in my camp, trainee, only assiduity. What's *assiduity*, trainee?"

"Sir . . . Trainee Rodríguez doesn't know, sir."

Jackson shook his head. "Look it up sometime. You're

going to need it. Fine, you wanna quit, go ahead, quit. See if your girl wants to be with a quitter. Go ahead."

Dio caught his breath. He couldn't move. Jackson just looked down on him and shook his head as he walked away. Fire burned in Dio's eyes. He couldn't stop. He wasn't going to let Jackson get the best of him. That motherfucker didn't know the half of what Dio was capable of doing. And he was going to show him. He just kept going, kept cranking out those pushups until he finished every last one.

Jackson about keeled over as Dio hopped up and stood at attention. "Sir, Trainee Rodríguez is finished, sir."

Jackson even arranged to give Dio an extra spamburger that day.

Dio's bunk never felt so good. He was so tired he couldn't even think. But a warm smile spread over his face as he realized what he had done. He'd succeeded. He'd actually succeeded at something and didn't quit. He wasn't a quitter. And he wasn't going to let Jackson get the best of him.

He knew Jennifer would have been proud. She always said he had so much potential. Somehow, in his own weird way, he felt he was one step closer to becoming somebody. He didn't know who or what yet, but something, someone better, someone stronger. And he was going to turn out a heap better than most the trainees. From that point on, every night before he said his prayers and went to bed, he was reading the dictionary, learning new words. It was boring, but anything was better than being treated like an idiot by Jackson.

"Rise and shine, Radigez!" Jackson yelled in Dio's face. It seemed like he had just closed his eyes when dawn hit. He couldn't move. His body felt like an old bucket that needed to be warmed up first.

But Dio did manage to get up. He had a new fire inside him to succeed.

Dio had been so busy that day he was surprised when Jennifer's letter came in. Before Dio could even tear the letter open, Simon was at his side.

"That from your lady?"

"Yep."

"What'd she say? What'd she say?"

He was as anxious as Dio to hear.

"Can you read it to me?" Simon asked.

Dio tried to hide his smile.

"Just hold up, man."

He tore the letter open, crossed himself, and said a little prayer before he read it.

"Dear Dio,

"That letter was really sweet thank you, so was the picture you drew of me. You're so talented. It meant a lot to me. Sorry I didn't make it to your Visitor's Day. I really am but I had to go back into the hospital since I started bleeding internally again.

"I'm sorry to see you in camp, I am but it's no easier for me in here. They say I might be able to get out of the hospital in another week. My mom's been here just about every day so has my dad and my hermanita—"

"What's that mean? What's that mean?" Simon asked.
"*Hermanita* is little sister."
"Oh, okay."
"Anyway, as I was reading . . .

"It's funny this whole thing has brought my familia all together again. My mom even read to me like when I was little. She has this permanent worried face all the time and she's always on my side practically day and night. She looks like she belongs in a hospital too. Her hairs all raged and everything. Dad practically has to drag her away just to pee. She always wants to be by my side.
"They want me to come home Dio. Both mom and dad. Can you believe it? They want me to get better at home and I think I might go. I almost cried when my mom said that. You know your padres care, I mean that's automatic but sometimes you've just got to hear it. Tu saves? Sometimes you just want to lay your head in your mom's lap while she brushes your hair and you just want to cry there like when you were little. I kind of need that now. I really do."

"I know how that goes," Simon added.
"Man, you going to let him read the letter or not?" someone yelled.
Dio looked up and noticed that everyone was listening in. Suddenly he felt all exposed, but he kept reading.

"I'm kind of worried cause I don't want the problems we had before. I don't want all the gritos. I don't want to feel like I want to run away again. I just get this feeling maybe it'll be different this time. Maybe things will change. I hope so cause I don't have no where else to go.

"I told you my big dreams Dio. I believe in them still I do. It's just it gets so hard out there alone with no place to call your own. I get tired of depending on other people. And I want to go to school again. I want to be somebody. Just for me, more than anything. I want to be like a responsible member of society. I don't want to be some puta anymore. I don't want people treating me like I'm just some nalgas. I'm more than that you know.

"Mom and Dad I never told them what I did out there on the streets to survive. I couldn't. It would break there hearts. But still I think they know. Somewhere inside I think they know but they block it out so they don't have to think about it.

"I even called Wiggie. Told him I'm not working for him anymore. I put star 67 so he didn't know where I was calling from. Scared me to death, I was shaking. But I had to do it. It's the only way I can move forward. I was scared but Dio, it felt so good. It felt like I was powerful again. Like now I can move on."

"What kind of job was that? Who's Wiggie?" Simon asked.

Dio's heart jumped to his throat. "Don't worry about it. You going to let me finish this letter, or not?"

"She's a hooker, dummy," Grossaint said. "That's what it sounds like."

Dio stood up. "Shut the fuck up, Grossaint."

"Why? It's true, isn't it? Wiggie's probably her pimp."
The guys looked at Dio for an answer.

Dio remembered that day, that very special day. He and
Spooky were cruising the streets downtown, looking for a
piece of ass basically. Now Spooky and Dio could pretty
much get any girl they wanted, and they pretty much had,
but Spooky had a taste for street hookers, a thirst for them
he couldn't quench.

It was about dusk, in the summertime, and they knew all
the hookers would come out—tall ones, thick ones, transves-
tites, whatever you wanted, you could have. Dio had his eye
on a little petite one, "Bounceable," Dio joked. She hardly
wore any makeup, her clothes were tight, and her dress practically went up to her belly button. She had this tough look
to her, but it only seemed to mask how nervous she must
have been. She had to be new at this. She had a natural
beauty, almost an innocence, that you didn't see much on
the streets. Dio squinted, looking hard. There was something
familiar about her. Then it occurred to him.

"Shit, pull over," Dio said.

"What?"

"Come on, man."

They pulled up to her and Dio rolled down his window.
She poked her head in.

"Hey, sweeties," she said, chomping on gum, "how you
feeling?"

"Jennifer?"

Her mouth dropped and she turned pale. "How . . . ? Oh, my God, Dio?"

She looked completely different. Gone were the nerdy glasses and flat chest, replaced by this gorgeous, beautiful, shapely Latina. If it weren't for her beautiful, indisputable eyes, Dio would have never recognized her.

"You two know each other?" Spooky asked.

"Get in," Dio said, opening the door for her.

"I . . . my boss, he'll . . ."

"No, we'll pay ya and you don't even have to do anything."

"What? You crazy, *ése?*" Spooky blurted.

Jennifer got into the backseat, and they didn't shut up all the way back to Spooky's place. They must have talked for hours, because when Dio turned around, he realized Spooky must have left the two of them alone and gone inside his house.

"Shit, I'm going to get busted," she said.

"What are you doing on the streets?"

She looked away. "It's just for a little bit, just 'til I can get on my own feet again."

"Your parents still acting a foo'?"

"Haven't talked to them in four years. What about you?"

"Same," he said, "I live with her now, have for the past six months. She's still a bitch. Always will be. Sad, but true."

"That's too bad."

"You still sing?"

"Yep, going to get my demo together soon, too, in just a few more months, soon as I get enough together."

He looked at her beautiful face. There was so much pain and sadness on it. It was weird seeing her so much older, but she'd gotten much more beautiful.

"Baby, you don't have to do this shit. You're too good for it. You need money, I've got tons."

"What are you doing? Robbing banks?"

"Nah, just providing for the community." He smiled.

"Still dealing?"

"Where else can you make this kind of money at seventeen?"

She looked at him and didn't say a word. He knew what she was thinking. This was not what they had planned for either of their lives.

"Still banging?"

"I'll always be down with my crew."

A look of terror flashed in her eyes. "What time is it? I better get back."

"Here." He handed her a wad of cash. "Stay with me tonight."

She tossed the money back and got out.

"No, you don't have to do nothing," Dio explained, "that's not what I mean. I just, you don't have to do that shit anymore. I'll take care of you."

"I don't need some man to take care of me, Dio. I survived this long without anyone. I'll do just fine."

She'd always been hardheaded. He knew that. But she was such a classy girl; he hated to see her like that.

"Please, just for the night."

As she turned around, her hair flirted with his heart. She could have been a teen model if she wanted to be.

"I missed you, you know," she said.

"Me, too."

He scrounged through his pants and found a scrap of paper to write his number on. Not finding one, he used a fifty-dollar bill.

She sighed.

"It's my cell."

She rolled her eyes. "I told you I won't accept any of your money."

"Take it."

She stuffed it in her bra and kept walking. "Only 'cause it has your number on it."

"At least let me drop you off," he said.

"I'll take the bus back."

—

"See?" Grossaint said. "He doesn't want to talk about it 'cause it's true. All Mexican women are hookers or wannabe hookers."

"Shut the fuck up," Dio blurted.

Coffee started barking at him.

"Shut up, you damned dog," Dio said. Dio didn't understand why anyone could even like Grossaint sometimes, even a damned dog. Ever since Grossaint's brother visited him, he seemed to be on a trail of vengeance. He seemed to hate the very ground Dio was standing on more than ever. There was so much hate in his eyes. Dio didn't understand how someone could have that much hate in his heart.

"I'd be pissed, too, if my girlfriend was a hooker."

Grossaint's cronies chuckled.

Dio couldn't get over to him fast enough. His fist was going to slam into him so hard . . .

"Officer on deck."

Dio stood at attention with everyone else as Jackson approached.

Did he see what just happened? Dio wondered.

He swallowed hard, catching his breath. His attention was split between Grossaint and Jackson prowling the line. He just eyed everyone, cleared his throat, and stopped in front of Grossaint.

"Grossaint, Radigez, Vifquain, come with me."

They all looked at one another, equally worried.

"Move it!" Jackson commanded. They obeyed as he headed out the door and then stopped.

"Well . . . ?" he said.

They looked at one another with confusion.

"Get the boxes," he barked.

Dio looked behind him. There were about twenty boxes stacked in front of their tent. He grabbed a couple of them and the guys did the same.

"Everyone, let's go!" Jackson told the rest of the squad. He led them to a big wooden trailerlike building, a hooch.

It was pitch-dark inside, but as Jackson flicked the light

on Dio could see it was jam-packed with bunks. A smile spread across Dio's face as he realized what was happening.

"Make sure you get all your things over here," Jackson said.

Dio and the guys couldn't open up the boxes fast enough. They each pulled out their new striped outfit, the second level. It looked like a jailbird suit, but Dio didn't care. He knew it was one step closer to graduating and one step closer to getting the hell out of there and back to Jennifer.

Had Jackson come in any later, he probably would have been at Grossaint's throat and neither of them would have been promoted. Sometimes Dio wondered if maybe there was a God, or maybe an angel looking over him.

Dio carried the rest of his things and shoved them into his personal trunk. Everyone got one. He sat back down on his bed and crossed himself, said a little prayer, and took the rest of Jennifer's letter out of his pocket to read.

They assigned this social worker to me. He's been really sweet brought me some green tea as a joke on St. Patrick's Day's. Everyone's been sweet even friends I haven't seen in years have come to see me. It's kind of funny. If I knew all this was going to happen I would have got shot a long time ago. Just kidding.

Be good okay. Hang tough. You'll make it.

Love,
Jennifer

She was always so positive with him. He was glad Jennifer was more upbeat. She was starting to sound like her old self again, which gave him hope. Dio drifted off to bed, fantasizing about being back out, spending time with her. He missed her so much.

Chapter Four

"Of course she wrote you back. I told you I knew what I was talking about," Louise said.

Dio was practically hopping up and down with excitement.

"Look, a woman knows," she added.

"I started writing her back. Wanna hear it?"

"Go ahead. But hurry up, you've got work to do."

"Yes, ma'am."

She tried to hide her interest as she stirred the pot of soup, listening intently to his letter.

Dio cleared his throat.

"Dear Jennifer,
  "Today I had to help the squad out—"

"Wait—wait—wait. Is that what you're going to say to her?"

Dio's eyes searched for a good answer, but, not finding one, said, "Yeah. Why not?"

"Hmm," she said, adding more salt.

She just kept on cooking. Finally, Dio couldn't take it anymore.

"What's wrong with it?"

She put the wooden spoon down, just itching to tell him.

"Well, all you're talking about is yourself. What about her? What about how she's feeling? She wants to know you care."

Dio thought for a while, then started writing. After a few minutes he read some to her.

"Hey baby thanks for the compliments. I'm glad you're feeling better. You sound much better.

"Hey maybe things will get better with you and your parents, you never know. I wish I could say the same for my moms. You're lucky. But just don't let them make you think anything about me that's not true cause you know who I am. They don't.

"I believe in your dreams too Mija. I know it. I know it in my everything baby. You're going to be big, grande and I'm going to buy all your rolas.

"I'm proud of you for standing up to Wiggie. He ever touches one hair on your head y le doy en su madre! Pinche socroso. But we won't have to worry about him anymore cause—"

"Wait a minute, wait a minute. Now, who's Wiggie? You lost me," Louise said.

Dio stared at the floor. "Her . . . pimp."

"Her what? You seemed to gloss over that tiny little fact. Jennifer hooks?"

"Hell no, not anymore. She got out of it. Don't judge her."

"I'm not. I just wondered."

"She's not just some stupid street hooker. She had a hard life. It was the only thing she could do to survive. I know her."

"I know you do. I wasn't judging her. I used to volunteer at the halfway houses. I know what those girls go through. Most of them are bright girls, just been through a lot."

Dio got lost in his thoughts. He had to admit it was hard at first to even think about going out with someone who had hooked on the side, but that's what was so special about Jennifer and him. They could see beyond what other people could see. They saw the soul inside. They saw the real person.

Dio remembered the night when he and Jennifer sat on top of the monkey bars, just like they did when they were in junior high. The moonlight shone through the trees and there was nobody else around, just them. Dio remembered the first time he reached for her hand and she took his. It just felt so right.

She smiled. "I'm going to be a star one day, you know," she said.

"Yeah?"

"Really, I am. Just have to get enough together for my demo."

"I believe you," he said.

He hadn't heard her sing in years, but he didn't have to. Sometimes you just know things; you don't even have to see them. You just know.

"You still haven't cut your hair?"

"Nope."

"Just like Samson," they both said at the same time and laughed.

"I like it, though," she said.

"Like yours, too."

His hand reached for her soft hair and his finger brushed against her neckline, so soft. His thumb stroked her olive-colored shoulders and he looked into her seductive dark eyes and he knew, they both knew, they were in love.

"You're beautiful, you know."

She smiled. "Well . . . I try."

"You don't need to," he said, and kissed her. He tasted her bottom lip, their tongues playing tag lightly, his hot passionate breath driving her wild. She had to catch her breath afterward.

"Wow," she said, smiling.

A smirk spread across his face. "What?"

"You . . . you've grown up."

She looked at his pretty eyes. For a guy, he had curly eyelashes.

Why do guys always have the nicest eyelashes? she wondered.

"I hate my life, you know. I hate doing what I do," she said, breaking away.

"But you don't have to."

"I won't live with those . . . those other girls. I'm not like them. I don't trust girls anyway—that's why I don't have any girlfriends. And I won't live in some halfway house. People steal your shit."

"You can live with me. I'm sure my mom wouldn't mind."

"You're sweet, but I've got to make it on my own. I just hate the way people look at you when you're on the street. They think that's all you are, just some street whore. But I'm not. I'm not, Dio. People don't know. I had to get out of my parents' house. I had to."

Dio knew she was right. If it was anything like it was when they were little, he didn't blame her for running away again. Her parents would say awful things to her, things parents should never say to their children. They never did believe her when she told them that her uncle had raped her. They just called her a liar and a slut.

He could tell she was trying not to cry. He held her close and rubbed her shoulders.

"I tried so many times just to get a regular job, but without parental consent, without an address of my own, without decent clothes . . . and Wiggie, my . . . my pimp, he's so . . . so cruel, Dio."

"He ever hit you?"

She looked at him. "Worse than that."

"I'll kick his ass."

"No, no, don't. It will only make it worse. I promise. It's just for a few more months, then I'll have enough to be on my own for good and I'll be able to stop."

He lifted her chin with his finger and looked into her beautiful eyes.

"You're going to be a star, just like you said. I can feel it. Will you sing me something?"

She smiled through her tears. And out of her beautiful, luscious, red lips came this voice, this powerful melodic voice of an angel. She closed her eyes as she sang and a smile spread on her lips. She was good. She was damn good.

"Music is medicine, you know," she said.

"You ever listen to Marvin Gaye?"

"No. Who's that?"

"You're a singer and you don't know who Marvin Gaye is? You know, from Motown. Now that's some deep shit. We ought to go back to my place. I got some in my room."

"'Kay." She smiled.

~~~

"You going to finish reading that letter you wrote, or what?" Louise asked. Dio snapped back to reality and continued.

"... first thing I'm going to do when I get out is get us a place to stay together and it's not going to be in some shit hole either. It's going to be a nice place like in Summerlin or even the Lakes. I'm planning it all in my head. That's what I do to keep my mind off all that goes on here. They have us cleaning out all these calles outside in the middle of no where. There're places where there's hardly any cars so I don't see how it gets so messy. Makes me think twice about throwing shit out the window that's for sure.

"They have us going to school too. They say I'll be able to get my G.E.D. by the time I graduate from boot camp. Ain't that a *trip? And to think the teachers in school used to say I'd never graduate.*

Love
Playboy"

Louise seemed lost in his words.

"They thought you were stupid or something?"

"Pretty much."

"Did the same thing to me when I was growing up."

"Yeah?"

"Yep. Maybe you got a learning disability or something."

"What's that?"

"It's when you're real smart inside, but you think differently. Or you can't read as well or you can't focus. There's lots of different kinds. Both my daughters got it, too. They also got two hard heads. You ought to have your teacher or somebody test you for it."

Dio shrugged. *Maybe she was right.* Maybe that's why he had so many problems concentrating all those years in school.

"Well, any idiot can tell you're as bright as can be. What were they thinking?"

Dio smiled. "You think?"

"Of course I think."

"Jennifer was the only one back then that would say anything encouraging to me. I was thirteen and I was going to commit suicide. I'm serious."

"What? At thirteen? Just from the way your teachers were treating you?"

Dio nodded. "And my moms, just had me down all the time."

"Your mom, too?"

"Yep. She just didn't know what to do with me, that's all."

"She beat you?"

Dio laughed. "Guess you could say that."

"She abused you?"

Dio had a smirk across his face. "Doesn't matter. Was a long time ago."

"They send you to social services?"

"Foster homes? Shit. Not soon enough. Nobody believed me anyway. Mom had a way of hurting me without leaving much bruises. They just thought I was in fights and shit, and I was. I tried to tell one teacher once, but . . . then my mom found out."

Dio chuckled.

～

Dio remembered that day clearly. He was just thirteen.

"You stupid, stupid, stupid boy," his mom said, in a drunken stupor. He looked away, but she had him cornered against the wall. He could smell the tequila on her breath.

"You're trying to break up this family, aren't you?"

"No," Dio said.

She slapped him across the face sharply. "Liar."

He bit his lip, not giving her the pleasure of seeing him cry.

"What did you tell that teacher? Tell me!" she said at the top of her lungs.

"Nothing."

She grabbed him by the chin and shoved his face back against the wall. His head ached from it.

"I don't let little liars in my house, Dio. You want to be on the street again tonight? Huh? Let those bums you hang out with take care of you. See if they want you. 'Cause I sure don't."

Dio's nose flared. "Good, 'cause I don't want you either. You're a horrible mother."

Her hand came across his face so fast he didn't know what hit him. She didn't let up, over and over and over again, until he was on the floor in a fetal position.

She stopped suddenly, her hand quivering.

"*Que descanse en paz*, what would your father think?"

He hated when she said that. She knew it got to him. Even at the age of thirteen, he couldn't help but think that somehow he had failed his father.

~

"Why you laughing about it?" Louise asked.

Dio looked up at her. His eyes teared. He wiped them as quickly as he could with his sleeve.

"You still have a lot of anger inside of you, Dio. You've got to find a constructive way to get that out."

"Let's talk about something else. 'Kay?"

"You know none of that was your fault, don't you?"

He shrugged. "Yeah, I know."

"Can I just ask you one thing about that, Dio?"

"What?"

"Where's your mom now?"

"Who cares? Probably rehab again."

"She's on drugs?"

"No, drinkin'. Just hope my little brother's okay."

"You've got a little brother, too?"

"Yep." Dio smiled. "That's my little motherfucker, too. We all tight, too."

She smiled. "That's wonderful. Wish my daughters would get along every once in a while."

"I'm like his gladiator, don't let nobody mess with him. He's going to be a tough little man, too, when he grows up."

"Maybe Jennifer can take care of him once she gets home."

"Maybe. That's what Jen used to do when I was younger. Used to go over to her house and crash at her place whenever my mom took it too far. Got tired of my mom's yelling and screaming. She'd take me in, even when her parents didn't like it. We both had it hard, real hard."

"She was abused, too?"

"Not like fists and stuff, but . . . the things her parents used to say . . . put her down and shit, call her a whore. No wonder she ran away. We were best friends since we was little. Always had each other, always will. At least I hope."

He just looked at Louise awhile until she snapped back and realized she was staring.

"Hmm. Well, my life hasn't exactly been a bed of roses either, but one thing I learned is that in the long run, everything happens for the greater good."

"What's that mean?"

"I mean, even if things seem really awful now, there's always something good that comes out of it. You'll see. If you two weren't abused so much as kids, maybe you wouldn't have had much in common. Listen, if you two are soul mates, if that's what you got, Dio, you're lucky to have her. Hold on to it. Never let it go, 'cause you may not get another one."

She started stirring the pot again.

"I'd never want another one."

"Well, just don't settle. Trust me on that," she mumbled.

Dio watched her for a second, as she was lost in her thoughts again, stirring the pot.

"That what you did? Settled?" Dio asked.

She stopped stirring for a moment.

"Well, that's a nosy-assed question if I ever did hear one. Why you always gotta be so nosy all the goddamn time?"

"Well, you asked me all these nosy-assed questions and I can't ask you?"

Her stirring became more aggravated. She mumbled to herself, then stopped and threatened him with the wooden spoon.

"I will say this," she said. "Any man that don't appreciate what he got's gonna lose it one day. That's why I say you show her you care about her. You treat that woman right. Show her she's secure in your arms. That's what you do and she won't have no reason to run off. Now get back to work."

Dio obeyed. He wondered what her life must be like. He figured her husband must have treated her pretty badly or she wouldn't have made those comments.

He was just glad to have someone to talk to, to give him advice from a woman's perspective. He wished his mom could have been the type, but she never was. Well, maybe not *never was*. Things were different before his dad got killed. But that was then, and after that she was a different person.

Dio waited until she left the room, then he added more to his letter. He was too embarrassed to read it to Louise, but he couldn't help but tell Jennifer a little bit about her.

They have me working in the kitchen, lavando platos and shit and you know how I hate that but I met this real cool mujer named Louise. Es bien suave, at first I thought she was just white trailer trash but I got to know her better and she always gives me good advice. She's kind of like a aunt or a mom or something to me. She gots no teeth in the front and her hairs all stringy but it's funny after you get to know her, she's nothing like she looks on the out-side. She's like this beautiful person. She's soft inside but hard on the outside. I guess kind of like me sometimes.

She's been through a lot of shit I can tell. She doesn't talk much about her home life. She acts real tranquila about it but I can just tell. She seems real triste sometimes. She's got problems with her hijas or something.

Seems like everyone here gots some drama. Even Simon, you know that tirile I told you about? The mulatto one? Found out his family has a grip of feria, but he's got the same problems I do. His parents don't want him either.

I miss you baby. I need you. I can't wait to hold you again and to smell you. That's what I miss the most about you. Sounds dumb but it's true. I miss the smell of your hair and kissing your soft lips. That's what I imagine before I go to bed every night. I think about you. About us.

Oh, before I forget. I got good news. Guess what? Our whole squad just got promoted to the next level. Just one more level to go, dark squad then we're out of here.

By the way, is there any way you could have somebody spend some tiempo with Daniel? He don't really got nobody he can play with in our hood. I just don't want him hanging out with the wrong people and getting in with the wrong crowd you know? I know your parents live in a much nicer area maybe if he can at least see that there's better things out there for him, that life don't have to be in the barrio, maybe he'll turn out all right.

I worry about him. And my mom's not exactly the best influence on him. You know? Hope you can help.

Love,
Playboy

"Get a move on!" Jackson blurted.

Dio looked to his side, where Grossaint was gaining on him. They were about to face the last wall in the obstacle course and Dio was actually in the lead. He climbed the wall, almost losing his footing. He landed with a thump, his heels aching from the hard desert floor, and started toward the hurdles, one after the other. Dio had never run faster in his life. He was lost in himself, just him and the world, with Grossaint as a distant memory as he burned up the rope— one hand over the other; finally he touched the top and slid down as Grossaint was just halfway up it.

Dio gave him a wink and raced to the finish. Jackson clicked on the stopwatch.

"9:03."

He seemed dazed by the time Dio had made. The squad cheered him on. He cleared his throat.

"All right, all right. Don't get too excited. Not bad, Radigez. Not bad."

Grossaint raced up to Jackson.

"9:47."

"Sir, Trainee Grossaint requests permission to speak," Grossaint said.

"Go ahead."

"Sir, Trainee Radigez didn't touch the top of the rope all the way. He's supposed to—"

"Who's the senior officer here, Grossaint?"

"Sir, you, sir. But—"

"But nothing."

"Sir—"

"But nothing!" Jackson barked. "Stop being so petulant. What is *petulant*, Grossaint?"

Grossaint looked at him, dumbfounded. "Sir, I . . ."

"No, no, and no! Not, 'Sir, I.' What is it, Grossaint? Haven't you been doing your studies?"

"Sir, yes, sir. But—"

"Sir, Trainee Rodríguez requests permission to speak, sir."

"Go ahead."

"Sir, *petulant* is an adjective meaning moody, ill-tempered, and whiny."

"That is correct, trainee. You ought to follow Trainee Radigez's lead, Grossaint, and get to your studies. There are no excuses in life, Grossaint."

Dio smiled at Grossaint.

"Yeah, there are no excuses in life, Grossaint."

"That's so gay. Oops, sorry, Simon," Grossaint said, sitting on his bunk.

Everyone laughed. Dio watched Simon shrink into his shell. He nudged him.

"Say something."

But Simon just stared at the floor.

"Why do you let him knock you like that, homes?"

Simon shrugged.

"You can't just let him push you around. Gotta stick up for yourself."

Grossaint sashayed down the aisle with a limp wrist. "Heeeeey! I'm Simon."

They all chuckled.

Dio rose. "Shut the fuck up, Grossaint, unless you like walking around like that."

Grossaint burned red. "Just look, Simon's little butt-boy has come to the rescue. What's up with you and him, anyway? You fags or something?"

"Why? 'Cause I stick up for my friends 'stead of talking about everybody behind their back like you?"

"Whatever, dude."

"You're just pissed 'cause I kicked your ass on the course again," Dio said.

Everyone laughed and Grossaint looked pissed.

"Yeah, you're just pissed 'cause he beat you," Simon added.

"Shut up, faggot."

"I know you are, but what am I?" Simon taunted.

Everyone froze. Did they hear what they thought they heard?

Oh, my god. What a nerd, Dio thought.

Dio sank into his bunk. He shook his head, feeling embarrassed for Simon.

"Sticks and stones, homie," Simon added, "sticks and stones."

Dio called Simon through gritted teeth. "Dude, sit down and shut up."

Simon obeyed.

"What?" he asked innocently.

"Sit . . . down."

"Why? What'd I say?"

Dio just shook his head.

Grossaint laughed. "What a fucking loser."

Everyone roared with laughter and Simon shrank back into his shell.

"You've been awfully quiet today," Louise commented.

Dio scrubbed around the tables with a small brush, drowning himself in hip-hop from the radio.

His mind was on the awful dream he kept having over and over again about Acne and Dirty Blond. They were always laughing in his face. "Don't want to fuck with me, spic." And he kept seeing Jennifer being shot, over and over again, her body flying through the air, her head hitting the pavement hard.

He didn't even notice Louise was there until she shut the radio off.

"What's going on with you?"

"Huh?" Dio said, waking out of his daze. "Oh, nothin'. I'm just, just thinking."

"About what?"

"Just nothing."

"Nothing? Still haven't heard back from Jennifer?"

"Not really."

In fact, the only letter he'd gotten was from his mom, and he didn't even bother opening that one. What could she possibly say? Call him stupid or irresponsible or a hundred other awful things she liked to say to him?

"How long's it been?" Louise asked.

"Like three weeks. I hate when she does this."

"Well, maybe she's busy."

"Too busy for me? I don't think so."

"Got to give her the benefit of the doubt."

"I guess."

"I used to get on my daughters' cases all the time. Didn't

understand why they were always coming home so late at night, or not at all. Used to think they were nothing but a bunch of rebellious teens. Then I learned to give them the benefit of the doubt, after some family therapy and things, and I realized . . . they just didn't want to be around me."

"How come?"

"Don't know, really. Always tried to be the best mother I could. Wasn't easy with all that was going on in the house. I guess they were mad at me 'cause they just didn't understand why I didn't leave my husband sooner."

"Why didn't you?"

She shrugged. "Sometimes you just get used to it, used to all the drama. Besides, he's changing. In fact, I gotta go meet up with him tonight."

"You gotta? . . . Sounds like love to me."

"Put up with a man like that for twenty-two years and you'd 'gotta' do a lot of things."

"Where you going?"

"His place."

"His place?"

"Yeah. We're spending some time apart for a while. He got tired of being thrown out on the couch."

"You guys never hook up no more?"

"Excuse me?"

"You know, mess around, make love."

"That's none of your business."

"Then when you getting a divorce?"

"I'm not getting a divorce. You don't listen very carefully, do you? I said we're spending some time apart."

"That's just fancy talk for eventually getting a divorce. . . . Divorce is a sin you know, says it in the Bible."

She grunted. "Good to know."

Louise was silent for a while.

"You still love him?" Dio asked.

"Course I do."

"He your true love?"

"We've been married for twenty-two years, haven't we?"

"Yeah, but being stuck with someone for twenty-two years just 'cause you're used to them don't mean they your true love."

"Never mind me. You just mind your own business. That reminds me, I almost forgot."

She ran back into the kitchen and handed him a book.

"What this?"

"Maya Angelou."

"What's that?"

"It's an author. And you oughta start reading her if you want to learn some romance."

"I don't need to learn no romance."

Louise snickered. "Is that so? Listen, she's a poet, and nothing reaches a woman's heart like poetry. Well, that and chocolate."

Dio laughed. "Poetry. I don't read that shit."

"Watch your language. And why not?"

"'Cause I don't. We got enough to read in class."

"You don't read 'cause you gotta; you read 'cause you wanna."

"Why would I wanna?"

"I just told you. Just read it. Make you a bet. You read about twenty of them pages in that book and if you don't see the point by then, you won't have to clean out the grease traps for a day."

A smile spread across his face.

"Don't give me that look, Dio. You better read it."

"All right, all right."

"I got your word?" she asked.

"Sure. Yeah. How you know all this stuff, anyway?" Dio asked.

"College."

"You went to college?"

"What do you mean, 'You went to college?' Course I did. Almost graduated, too, just a semester away."

"Why didn't you finish?"

Louise seemed to struggle with an answer.

"Things come up, some things more important than college. Anyway, why would you not think I went?"

Dio didn't know how to put it, but the truth was, you looked at Louise and she was the last person you'd imagine would have gone to college. She talked like she was from the sticks.

Weren't college-educated people supposed to be polished and professional-looking?

"I don't know," Dio lied. "Just wondering."

"I'll have you know I was at the top of my class. University of Kansas West. Not far from where Senior Jackson grew up, actually. Was going to be a psychologist and everything."

"A shrink? You would have been good at that."

"Yeah?"

"Yeah, 'cause you're always asking all them questions and you listen real good, too."

She smiled. "Well, thanks. You could go to college if you wanted. You're smart enough. You keep at your studies and keep your nose clean and out of trouble, you could go far."

"Me? Nah. I got a family to feed once I get out of here," Dio said.

"You can do both, you know. I did for a while."

"I don't know."

"What would you study, if you went?"

Dio was lost in his thoughts, and then he smiled. "I don't know."

"Come on, tell me."

"I don't know. I like art. Jennifer always thought I was good at it. And sometimes when I was little, we'd sneak into the museum downtown. You know, the one by the library?"

"Leed or Lied, or whatever it's called?"

"Yeah."

"Well, part of being an artist is reading. Poems, literature, that's just another way of expressing yourself."

Dio squinted and then smiled. Out of the blue he said, "You're in love with someone else 'sides your husband, aren't you?"

"What?" Louise demanded. "What makes you think that?"

"I can just tell. Someone else got your heart. Maybe someone long ago."

"We've all had crushes in the past."

"But this one's different. I can tell. You loved him. And he loved you. You ever look him up?"

"I couldn't just look him—you know, you sure are one nosy little bugger."

"Why not? You're gonna get a divorce."

"I'm not going to get a—"

"Well, you're going to be single soon. Why not look him up?"

"That's enough of all this chit-chat today. Get to work."

And she headed right back into the kitchen.

Dio wondered why she pushed away any time he asked her something personal. What was so private that she couldn't talk about it? Sure, maybe it was against boot camp policy, but they'd crossed those boundaries a long time ago. They were more than just employer and employee; they were friends. He knew that. He trusted her and there was a part of her that trusted him, too. It'd been a long time since he could trust anyone besides Jennifer and now he'd met two, Simon and Louise.

Dio drew another portrait of Jennifer. They didn't give him much to work with, no colors, just a plain old pencil, but in his mind she was full of color and full of life.

He sighed; he knew he was supposed to read that damn book of poetry. He had promised Louise, and a promise was a promise. It was bad enough having to go to school in camp every day or having to read the dictionary at night. At first it was a dread. He didn't even understand most of it, but then, the more he read, the more he got into it. The more he got into it, the more he enjoyed it. And the more he enjoyed it, the more he connected to what she was saying in the book. That night he read half the book. He just couldn't put it down.

~

"What'd she say?" the trainees asked.

Dio sighed. Another night and he knew they'd never leave him alone unless he read Jen's letter to them, so he did.

"Dear Dio,

"I haven't been feeling all too good lately. It's hard enough for me to get out of bed and go to the kitchen let alone out of the house. I don't have a car and there's no way in hell I'm going to ask my parents for a raite. It seems like my mom's starting to be like her old self again, which is not a good thing. She came into my room today and insisted I have some picture of Jesus on the wall and not only that but she wanted it in a certain spot. She got all bitchy when I said 'whatever.' I just pray it's not a sign that things are going to be like they were before.

"It's so weird here it's like all our history, all the things we've been through are in the pared. They're in my cama. They're on the techo and I can't escape it. The only thing that keeps my mind off of it is watching TV so I sit in the bed most of the time and just watch novelas, and then comes the stupid cartoons which I'm starting to actually like and then all the talk shows and the boring news. Most of the time I just sleep. It gets so boring.

"Oh, I just wanted to let you know that I had the social worker pick up Daniel and bring him over to me. He remembered me. I try to give him things to do and now he and Desiree have started to play together. Most of the time se estan peleando and my mom just screams at them to stop. I think it's funny actually. At first mom didn't want him around Desiree at all. It was like she felt some how your old bad habits would rub off on her someway but now I think Mom kind of likes it. It gives her like a sense of purpose or something. She feels like a mother over again. That's what I think.

"That reminds me Daniel said that your mom's actually going to AA right now. Isn't that great? That's a good start, isn't it? Seems like you're not the only one making changes. Wouldn't it be nice if she became like she was before when you were a little chavalillio?

"Well ya me voy a hir. I've been spending more time on the pot than anything lately. And I've got this rash and I'm always feeling hot, must be the medication. Talk to you later OK. Be good.

Love,
Jennifer"

"Sounds like she's spending a lot of time with that social worker guy of hers," Franklin said, snickering.

"Yeah, sounds like you might have some competition," Grossaint said.

The squad laughed. Dio was pissed. Not so much that

they had said it, but that they had said it in front of everyone.

"Hey, you're not giving it to her, somebody else will," Grossaint said, laughing. "That's what skanks do."

Dio pulled out a drawing of her. "Does she look like a skank to you? I don't think so."

"That's a fake," Grossaint said. "You couldn't get a girl that good."

"Fuck you, motherfucker," Dio answered. "Like to see the toothless girl you got."

Everyone laughed, but it still didn't heal the wound Grossaint had made in him.

What an asshole, Dio thought.

But he wondered, *Could they be right?*

He held on to the letter and kept reading it over and over again the next day, as if it would give him some answers. But it didn't. Dio stuffed the letter in his back pocket as he helped Simon weed the garden. Jackson had made them all start planting flowers and herbs and vegetables and things about a week before. He said something about it helping them learn patience, whatever that was supposed to mean. But Dio had to admit, there was something about gardening he kind of liked. It was like connecting to nature, or maybe it was because he just liked the thought of building something from scratch and seeing it grow. Whatever it was, it was peaceful.

Dio looked at Simon. Strange, he didn't ask any questions or anything during the letter. In fact, it seemed like he wasn't even listening.

"*Qué pasa*, homie?"

"Huh?"

"S'up," Dio said.

"Oh, nothing. I'm just thinking."

"'Bout what?"

"About life."

Dio looked at Simon. He didn't seem to be all the way there. It must have been the heat or something.

"You all right, man?"

Simon smiled a silly smile. "Doing fine," he answered.

"Maybe you should step out of the sun for a while. I think it's getting to you."

"Why does Grossaint hate me?"

Dio shrugged. "He's just an asshole. That's all."

"No, it's more than that. He likes picking on me. He hurts me when you're not around."

"What?"

Simon had trouble making his words come out. His lips started trembling. "He does. And I try to make him stop, I do. Honest, I do, but nothing I do . . ."

Simon thought back to the first time he had interacted with Grossaint. It was only the first day or so of camp. He watched Grossaint and his friends from around the corner of the main building. They were sanding down the wood of an old fence. They seemed to be laughing, quietly of course, so as to not let Jackson know. If they hadn't been in prison garb you could have sworn they were just a bunch of teenage boys goofing off at work.

"No, I'm serious. I'm going to do it, too," Grossaint told the others. "Soon as I get out of here, gonna get a job with my cousin out in Pahrump. If I get into the union, I can be making thirty to forty dollars an hour making cabinets for casinos and shit."

"That much?" Franklin asked.

"Yeah. That's what my dad did before . . . before he got laid off. But now there's more jobs than before. You two can come with me, too. You have to do some tests and shit to get into the union, but even you knuckleheads could handle it."

They laughed.

"Best of all, hardly any trouble out there either. Just good ol' hard-working Americans, families and shit trying to make a livin'."

"Yeah?"

"Yeah. There's only like fifty thousand people out there anyway. How much trouble could there be? They've got jobs lined up for union workers, too. 'Sides, there are more good, quality women out there than the skanks in Vegas."

They laughed again.

"Man, the girls out here make me itch," Grossaint joked.

They roared with laughter. Simon couldn't help but laugh, too. They seemed like pretty cool guys, down to earth. They even seemed to have woman trouble just like he did, or at least just like he wished he did. He hadn't really connected with anyone by then, so he figured he might approach them.

He cleared his throat.

"Hey," he said, his voice all squeaky, as usual.

They looked at him, then looked at one another. Something was brewing in their minds and Simon didn't know what.

"I'm Danny. Danny Simon."

"Who gives a fuck who you are, nigger?" Grossaint said.

The others chuckled.

It was as if someone had shoved a dagger in his heart. It shocked the hell out of him. It just didn't seem like the same guys he had seen goofing off.

He backed away.

"What the fuck do you want? Get out of here," Grossaint said.

Simon backed off. It was just like junior high school. The popular kids separated from the nerds; only there was no one else for him to hang with.

"Find you trying to talk to us again and you'll find yourself lynched up some tree," Grossaint said.

"Or dragging behind some truck," Franklin added, laughing.

"*Chale*, homes. You can't let him walk all over you like that," Dio said, putting his garden tools down. "You gotta fight."

"I don't know how."

Dio looked to see if anyone was watching, then pulled Simon over to the side by the laundry buildings. He started throwing punches into the air. Simon winced.

"Man, don't back up like that. You gotta fight back. Hold up your fists."

Simon obeyed, but looked like he was afraid of his own fists. Dio showed him how to hold them, how to jab, how to duck, but he was getting it all wrong. Finally, Dio sighed.

"You gotta jab," Dio said, throwing a punch at the wall. "You gotta—" but Dio's fist went right through the plaster wall. Simon gasped.

"My bad," Dio said, cracking a smile.

He peered through the hole and could see right through to the other end of the laundry building.

"Senior Jackson wants us to head out."

Simon and Dio turned around. Grossaint was behind them, with an evil grin on his face. He just looked at them, like he was up to something.

"He's going to tell. He's going to tell," Simon whispered.

"Chill. I'll handle it."

But he didn't tell. Two days went by and he still hadn't said anything. Dio wondered what he might be up to.

Dear Jennifer,

Thanks a lot for taking care of my little brother. I know he's in good hands now and I'm not so worried about him anymore.

Tease him about having a <u>girlfriend</u> for me won't you? He's always been volado. I remember being that age. He's going to be a player just like his big brother. I don't need to be a player no more. I got you.

As far as my mom, ~~I couldn't give a~~ I don't care about her. She tried to send me a letter but I threw it away didn't even bother opening it. What's she going to say that she hasn't already? It's all a bunch of bullshit anyway.

She always talks about quitting. This is no different. I think it's a bunch of pendejadas that she thinks she'll actually make it through. If it was up to me, I'd say she wasn't ever fit to be a mother. She was always thinking about herself. She'll be partying 'til the day she dies. She'd much rather be with her friends than raising us. She's always been like that. She'll always be.

Hey I was telling the guys here about you. They think I'm a tapado. I showed them the pictures I've drawn of you and they think I'm making you up. They say it's cause I talk about you like you're an angel or something and I tell them you are my angel.

Hang in there with your mom. I know it's not easy for you but just keep thinking about your sueños and keep thinking about how great it'll be when I'm out and I'm going to get a real job and I'm going to fix up a place for both of us and neither one of us will have to put up with any bullshit anymore.

Hope you feel better soon cause Visitor's Day's coming up again next week and I hope you can make it. Maybe that social worker guy you were talking about can take you. And can you bring Daniel with you too? I'd love to see him. I'd love to see both of you.

Love,
Dio aka Playboy

Patter-patter-boom. Patter-patter-boom. A smile curved up on Dio's face as he listened to the rhythmic beat of someone drumming in the pantry. Whoever it was was good, real good. Dio's jaw dropped as he turned the corner into the pantry and saw Simon pounding a real mean beat on the boxes. He froze as he saw Dio.

"Damn!" Dio said, smiling, "I didn't know you were a drummer."

Simon smiled bashfully. "Just something I do when I'm bored."

Dio snatched the carrot sticks from his hands. "How long you've played percussion?"

"I was in band in the sixth grade. It was the one thing I was good at. First time I ever found people I liked to hang with."

"You ought to do it for a living."

Simon smiled. "Thought about it. Dreamed about it, actually."

"Why don't you do it? I'm serious. Soon as we get out, I'll introduce you to my lady. She's going to need a drummer in her band, I'm sure of it."

"For real?"

"For real, man. And you got the skills."

"You think?"

"Man, would I say it if I didn't?"

Then a sadness came into Simon's eyes. "My parents would never allow it."

"Who cares what they think? When's your birthday?"

"Next December."

"You'll be eighteen next December. You'll be an adult. They can't tell you what to do then."

Simon smiled. "I like the way you think, Dio. You're lucky, you know. You got so much."

"You're the one with the money."

"I'm not talking about that. I'm talking about . . . I mean, look at you. You got the girl. You got the confidence. You got balls. You can talk to anybody. I've always been too black for the Latinos and too Latino for the blacks. I just never fit in."

"You gotta strut, *ése*. One thing I learned is that God made you just the way you're supposed to be. He don't make no mistakes. He made you half Mexican, half black for a reason. You got the beats from the black side, didn't you? You got the wavy hair from the Latino side. Soon as your zits clear up, you'll have all the ladies after you."

Simon nodded. Then he snapped out of the funk he was in and his eyes lit up. "So, I thought of something, some way we could get back at Grossaint."

"Again? What?"

"What we do is when he's in the shower next time and nobody else is around, we lock him in there and soap up the handles and the floors so he falls on his ass."

Dio cracked up until he realized Simon was serious.

"Man, why do you always need me to carry out your plans? You're the one that thought of that whole dog-shit-in-the-shoe thing. Why don't you do it sometime?"

Simon looked at the floor, "'Cause . . . you're my boy, ain't you? 'Sides, I'm not good at carrying things out. You are."

Grossaint was gaining on him. They were neck and neck up the ropes. Dio couldn't even hear all the cheers and hoopla from the squad. He was in the zone. He eyed Grossaint as he touched the top, but Grossaint was already on his way down.

Dio's hands burned as he slid down the rope and landed with a thud. He looked over at Grossaint, who was already steps ahead of him, and there was no way in hell he was going to let him beat him. Dio burned rubber.

They were again neck and neck, just a hundred feet from the finish, when Dio went into second gear and beat Grossaint by a nose hair. He raised his arms in the air and jumped up and down.

Jackson couldn't help but crack a smile. "Had trouble with that hurdle back there, didn't ya, Radigez?"

"Sir, yes, sir," Dio answered, out of breath.

"Well, ya gotta lift that leg, like I keep tellin' ya."

"Sir, yes, sir. I know, sir."

Grossaint glared as Jackson rubbed Dio on the head. "Good job," he added.

Dio looked at Grossaint. He looked lost and alone. Hardly anyone was paying attention to him at all. And for the first time since he arrived in camp, Dio felt sorry for him. Dio made his way over to him and extended his hand.

"Nice job, Grossaint," he offered.

But Grossaint just glared at him and walked off.

"Well, don't blame me," Grossaint said, as he walked back to the hooch with Franklin and his boys. "If y'all had pulled together on your end, we wouldn't have lost. My dad always said, 'You gotta be the best. This world ain't meant for losers.'"

"Dude, I did pull together. You're the one that let the fuckin' wetback win again," Franklin said.

"Yeah, well, he cheated again," Grossaint answered.

"You faggot," Franklin said under his breath.

Grossaint shoved him against a wall and pinned him on the ground, his fist in the air.

"I ain't a fuckin' faggot."

Franklin had terror on his face. "Dude, I was just jokin'. I'm sorry."

The guys had to pry Grossaint off him. Grossaint looked dazed as he realized what he had done. His fist trembled. He lowered it and loosened his grip on Franklin. "I'm . . . I didn't mean it."

But Franklin was too busy wiping his bloody nose.

"Brothers?" Grossaint said.

Franklin couldn't even look at him.

"Come on, man. We're still brothers, right?"

"That was not cool."

"Dude, come on. We're still brothers. Say we're still brothers. Come on . . . I just, sometimes, sometimes something happens in me and I just . . . sometimes my mind tells me to do things, and I have to fight, fight real hard not to do them. Know what I mean?"

Franklin looked at him strangely as Grossaint's eyes started to twitch. Then Grossaint started hitting himself on the head real hard. "Stop, stop, stop. I try, man. I try real hard." His eyes started to water. "But it just gets real bad sometimes, my mind, things it tells me to do. Sometimes I think I'm going to go nuts. Know what I mean? You gotta understand. We're still brothers, right? Right?"

"Yeah . . . yeah," Franklin said, still looking oddly at Grossaint.

"Can we keep it quiet down here?" Jackson asked the crowd of visitors.

Dio stood in line all alone. Everyone had guests except him; even Simon had a guest.

Simon's mom had shown up. She was a beautiful Latina woman, one of those high-society types. She looked at everyone like she was too good to be sitting in the same room and breathing the same air. She was wearing some fancy suit by Chanel or Gucci or one of those fancy labels and her hair looked like she had just stepped out of the most expensive salon in the city.

She was probably the most serious person in the entire room. Dio couldn't make out what she was saying to Simon, but he could tell he didn't like it. Every time he tried to say

something his mom would cut him off. He swore he heard
Simon say, "It's not fair!" but he couldn't be sure.

Grossaint was overwhelmed by all his foster brothers
and sisters. It was what Louise would have called ironic, Dio
thought, because not one white kid was among them. Grossaint's foster brothers and sisters were all black and Asian
and some were even retarded. Even his foster parents were
complete yuppies, not the type of parents Dio would ever
imagine for Grossaint. He had to chuckle a little as Grossaint kept trying to push the little rug rats away from him.

But, more than anything, Dio was sad because Jennifer
hadn't shown up like he had asked her to. He knew she
wasn't feeling up to it, but he really wanted to see her and
he really wanted to see his little brother. He'd hoped she
would have gotten somebody to bring her and drop her off
or something. There was no way she got the letter too late
or something, or got the dates mixed up again, not two
times in a row. She simply had decided not to come—that
had to be it. Louise always said to give people the benefit of
the doubt. Well, Dio was getting tired of doing that, tired of
being patient with people. What about him? What about
his feelings?

"Women don't make no sense," Dio told Louise. "One minute they up, next minute they not. You tell them their dress
looks fly, then they wonder why you didn't comment on
their shoes."

Louise laughed. "Touché," she said, "but men aren't any easier. Trust me on that."

She could see that Dio wasn't laughing, so she put her hand on his shoulder. "You have to understand the makeup of a woman. She needs understanding. She needs to know that she's secure. That's just the way that we are. Can't help it. Nothing makes us feel more up than knowing our man's there for us no matter what, even when we don't make any sense."

"Yeah?"

"Yeah. Try to see it through Jennifer's point of view. She just got out of the hospital. She's dealing with her mother and all the problems that go along with mother-daughter relationships. She just got shot, and if you're honest with yourself, you'd have to take some responsibility for that."

"I know," Dio admitted.

"So she's probably reevaluating her life. I believe that connection's real, the one that you told me you have with her. And I'm sure she feels it, too, but she's going to be eighteen soon and there are a lot of decisions she's going to have to make from this point on."

"Yeah, I know."

He hated to admit that she was right, but it was true. He just wanted her so bad and wanted her to feel all the things he was feeling. Whenever she didn't show up or didn't answer a letter right away, it just made him question whether she was feeling for him the way he was feeling for her. He hated the thought of ever losing her. And he didn't like the idea of seeing her go after all these years. They had been through so much together.

＝＝

Dio thought back to the night when he made that stupid decision that set everything into motion. He was sleeping peacefully in his room when he heard this *tap! tap! tap!* Dio woke up from his deep slumber and looked out the window to see Jennifer, tapping on his window. He sprang up and opened the window.

"What's going on?" he asked.

He took her hand and helped her through the window. Her mascara was running and she was in tears. She couldn't talk for at least ten minutes as he held her close, sobbing. He could see she had a big black eye.

"Wiggie do that to you?"

"I told him I was done. I told him I couldn't do it anymore. I told him how I had just got ahold of my parents and that I was trying to clean up my life, and he . . . just didn't like what I had to say."

Jennifer had just reached out to her parents after Dio's urging that she try to give them another chance. Family was important, and maybe they had changed after all these years. He was right. They welcomed her into their home with open arms and happy tears. It was nice to see Jennifer happy again. She had made the first step in turning her life around. He knew they wouldn't allow her to move back in unless she became a religious fanatic like them, but at least they let her in the house.

Rage filled Dio. He was about to break through the door and go after Wiggie when Jennifer pleaded with him.

"No, please don't. Stay with me tonight. Just hold me."

It surprised Dio. Jennifer never was the needy type. He loved being with her and loved holding her, but she'd always been so feisty, an "I-don't-need-no-man" type. So he knew if she was asking him to hold her, it had to be serious. It took him a long time to calm down. He did hold her all night, but his mind was on Wiggie and what he was going to do to him once he got hold of him.

"Hello! Hello, Earth to Dio," Louise blurted out, waving in front of Dio's face. "I said did you read any of the book I gave you?"

Dio's eyes lit up. "Yeah. They're not bad."

"See? I told you. Which one was your favorite?"

"All of them, pretty much. I've heard her talk on TV once, Maya Angelou, and I felt like I could hear her speaking while I was reading it."

As Dio worked at cleaning out the grease traps, he noticed Louise had a permanent grin on her face.

"Whatchew smiling about?" Dio asked.

She just kept on working. "I'm not smiling."

"Yes, you are. You were smiling from ear to ear."

"I was not," she said, trying to hide her grin. She got back to work, but then couldn't help herself. She had to say something. "I looked him up yesterday."

"Who?" Then it dawned on Dio. "That guy. That guy you loved."

"Well, I was just curious. You know, wondering how he was doing after all these years."

"How'd you find him?"

"Let's just say it helps to have friends that work at the DMV."

"What'd he say? What'd he say?"

She was grinning so hard that she looked ready to bust.

"He was real nice. It was like old times. We talked and talked and talked. Must have spent two hours on the phone."

"Two hours? *Simón*. See? That's the guy you supposed to be with, not some fuckhead."

"Watch your language. He's not a fuckhead. He's just . . . not always so easy to deal with. And besides, me and Sam are just friends. Just friends . . ." she said, staring off into the distance dreamily. "I think it's true, Dio. Sometimes it seems like maybe once in your life you'll meet that special somebody."

She laughed.

"He wants to take me to some club, La Soolsuh or something like that."

"La Salsa? I know where that is. He's taking you to a Latin club?"

"He says there's dancing and things. I'll just watch.

Sounds exciting. He's divorced, too. I mean, I'm not divorced, but you know, he's . . . we're both available right now."

Louise was lost in her thoughts, looking nervous. "I ought to just cancel. It's too soon. I'm not even officially separated yet."

"But you want to go, right?"

"I'm not ready. And my hair . . . I've got nothing to wear . . . and my teeth. He's never seen me looking this awful. Who'd want me?"

"Don't talk like that. I think you're beautiful."

"You do not. Stop that."

"You are. You can fix your hair. I know a lady downtown that does hair. She could fix you up real good. Just tell her you're my friend. She's cheap, too. And you can get a good outfit at Target or Savers or something. Probably only cost you like twenty bucks."

She looked at him endearingly, then she touched her hand to her mouth and her eyes started to water.

"But my teeth," she cried.

She sobbed, and Dio didn't know what to do. He came over to her and let her put her head on his shoulder. He made her look at him.

"You are beautiful, Louise. He don't see that, then he ain't worth your time."

She laughed through her tears, then sucked them up. "I can't do none of those Latin dances."

Dio turned the radio to a station that was playing Spanish music.

"I'll show you. Put your right arm out and your hand on my shoulder. This is merengue."

She shuffled and tripped through the first few steps, but then she started getting the hang of it.

"My mother may not have been good for much, but she did teach me to dance. Taught me all the traditional Mexican and Latino dances when I was little."

Louise smiled. "I like this. This is fun. Been years since I danced with a man." She laughed nervously. "You're probably the first person I've ever spent any time with that never asked me how I lost my teeth."

"I figured it was none of my business. That's all."

"Well, it was sweet of you."

She paused for a while, not sure exactly how to say what she needed to say. "Unfortunately, not all the men I've been around were so sweet. My lack of judgment has been awful. My mother used to get on me, picking all these losers and stuff. Men used to do awful things to me. Awful things," she said.

Dio knew what she was trying to tell him without her saying it.

"Your husband do that to you?"

She tried to laugh it off. "You'd think a college-educated gal would have more sense. You do me a favor. Promise me something."

"Sure. What?"

"You always treat that girl of yours good. You hear me?"

"Yes, ma'am."

"And . . . you give that mom of yours another chance."

"What?"

"We all make mistakes, Dio. Believe me. And sometimes,

well, parents always do the best they know how. Sometimes they make mistakes; Lord knows I have. Just give her one more chance. See what she wants. She do you wrong again, then you have every right to be mad. Do that for me, will you?"

Dio wouldn't look at her.

"Please?"

Chapter Five

Dear Dio,

I don't have a recent photo but here's a photo from about a
year ago with me and you together. I don't think you'd even want
to see me right now. I don't look like my old self. I'm gaining so
much weight lately and I don't feel like my old self either. I'm trying to stay up I really am. But sometimes it's such a struggle. I
mean I've always been the person who's lifted everybody else's spirits
up. And now I've got to lift mine. I don't want people to see me like
this. Lo odio. And I'm sick and tired of the looks of sympathy on
everyone's faces. They try to fake it, like I look normal like things
are the same but they're not. I try not to let them see how triste I've
been. I don't want them to see me like this and it takes so much energy to fake it, to force a smile. I'm tired of the visitors and I'm
tired of my mom bringing people over from the iglesia. All they do
is tell me the same scriptures over and over again about the "tiem-
pos finales" and how things will be better in "el reino de Dios."

I told my mom I just want to be solita, but she doesn't seem to
listen and I don't want to be rude to them. I feel like I'm trapped in

this bed Dio. I feel like I'm in the pinta. I feel like even though I could physically get up and leave and I know I could that I can't. That I'm emotionally trapped. And I want to get out.

I want to be myself. Quiero cantar otra vez. I've stopped watching Entertainment Tonight Dio, and you know that's my favorite show. You know why? Cause every time I watch it and I see some star on there and they're doing so great and they've got the perfect hair and the perfect smile and they're on the red carpet and they have some new album or new movie coming out I just can't help but think, "that's supposed to be me." And I want it so bad Dio. I want to be there and I know I can but I feel so trapped and I don't know how to get there.

Sometimes I wonder if I'll ever get better, if I'll ever be back to where I was. It seems so far away. The social worker comes over, his name is Angel. He always gets me laughing. And I hate it cause as soon as he's gone like an hour later my mom does something that pisses me off, or I just get this huge wave of doubt that hits me like a thick cloud and I'm back to where I was. I hate being lifted up and then I'm just dropped and it takes so much effort to just be lifted up again and for what? I'm just going to be dropped again? That's how I feel.

You know today is the anniversary of Marvin Gaye's death, April Fool's Day. Did you know that? I saw it on the news. I'm glad you introduced me to him. I've been reading about him lately. He left such a mark, and he felt so triste all the time. I wonder if he knew he was a legend or if he knew he'd make that much of an impact. It's funny sometimes people don't appreciate you until you're gone. I wonder if they'll appreciate me when I'm gone.

*I just don't want to leave this earth without making a mark.
I've got so much to tell Dio. I've got so much to say. I want to
scream it out but sometimes it feels so hard and I feel like I'll never
get there.*

*I'm sorry. I don't want to depress you. It's just you're the only
one I can tell this kind of thing to. You're the only one I can be
myself to all the time. I don't have to be perfect with you. I don't
have to be up. I can be real. I can be me.*

Thank you,
Love,
Jennifer

He hated to hear Jennifer down like that. She was right;
it wasn't like her. It must have been the medications that
were doing something to her mood. He wanted to be there
right then to just hold her and tell her everything was going
to be okay. He wanted to tell her all the exciting things that
were happening, all the changes that were happening to him
in camp. He was only a few months away from graduating
and Senior Jackson had even given him the responsibility for
laundry duty. Any other person outside the camp would have
considered it a chore, but everyone in camp knew it was a
privilege. He chose Dio out of the whole squad because he
said he "needed someone responsible." Dio had never been
trusted with anything before, and he was on cloud nine supervising everyone with the laundry.

Something occurred to Dio . . . Grossaint. Something
was troubling him about Grossaint and he couldn't put his
finger on it. True, he had to supervise him and he didn't

seem all that pleased lately. He seemed very quiet, avoiding eye contact with Dio, but always picking on Simon whenever he got a chance.

Dio couldn't always be there to protect Simon; that he knew for sure. And Simon was actually starting to get some *cojones.* But Simon always followed Dio around, everywhere he went. He was like a mini-Dio, really. He mimicked everything Dio did, how he said things, how he walked. He was like a little dog that would bark at all the big dogs, but only if his owner was around; otherwise Simon was defenseless.

Dio didn't mind sticking up for Simon, but he knew Simon had to learn to do things on his own. In just a few short months they were going to be graduating and they might never see each other again; then what would Simon do?

Dio stared at the picture she had sent him for hours. He rubbed his thumb over her picture, kissed it, imagined a million scenarios. They made a good-looking couple, everyone had always told them. They were like two peas in a pod, always inseparable, and it tore his heart out to be away from her for this long.

Dear Jennifer,

Baby don't let the world get you down, OK? You got to know who you are adentro. I know. I know you're going to be the biggest singer there is. I know you're going to be huge. I know you've got more talent in your pinky than most those stars have in their whole cuerpo.

All that's not real anyway. That's all smoke and mirrors. It's all makeup and lighting and suped-up, over-produced tracks, synthesizers

and shit. That's what it is. Without their professional beats and pro-
duction they sound like shit. And you're real. That's why you're going
to be huge. You got heart and people are going to feel it. They'll feel
it like I feel it. Like I've always felt it.

Don't ever talk about muriendo. If anything ever happened
to you I don't know what I'd do. I'd pull some Romeo & Juliet
shit I know. I can't bear thinking what it'd be like with you not
around. We're meant to be juntos baby. Better than Romeo &
Juliet. Better than any of those guys. Te amo. And as soon as I
get out I'm going to buy you the biggest bouquet of flowers and
I'm getting you candy and I'm getting you a shopping spree and
all that shit. I don't know how, but if I have to work at fuckin'
McCaca's night and day I'm turning both our lives around.
Don't you let anybody knock you down cause you eres mi inspi-
ración. You're my love.

You lift me up without even trying. I just think about your smile
and damn girl it just lights me up. Nobody does that like you to me.
Nobody.

You're going to make your mark just like Marvin Gaye did.
You're going to be bigger than him. I know it.

Just hold on baby, I'll be back before you know it. And
keep writing me as much as you can cause you lift me up. Every
time I get a letter from you it just picks up my day. The homies
always know whenever you've written me because I've got a permanent grin on my face for the whole day. Man I can't wait to
see you.

I love you baby. I miss you.

Love,
Dio

Simon and Dio spent most their free time talking about music, talking about Simon's dreams of becoming a drummer for a rock star, about how he dreamed of being in an MTV video just so his parents could see. Simon would pound out a dope beat and Dio would free-flow, usually something funny to crack them both up.

"My stepbrothers would be so jealous if I got on MTV," Simon said, his eyes looking up at the ceiling. "Man, I can see their faces for sure. Mark my words, Dio, I'll be famous one day. One day I'll be so big, nobody will forget me. I'll be so big, my parents won't even be able to get in to meet me."

"Excuse me," Dio said, mimicking a nasal voice. "Excuse me, I'd like to speak to Mr. Danny Simon, please."

"I'm sorry," Simon kidded, pretending he was a secretary, "Mr. Simon is unavailable at this moment. Can I take a message?"

"This is his father."

"Mr. Simon says he'd love to speak to you, but he's . . . too busy partying with Oprah and Donald Trump and the hoochie girls from P. Diddy's video."

They busted out laughing.

"That what you want? To be too busy for your parents?"

"Would serve them right, don't you think?"

Dio shrugged. "I guess so. But one day you're going to inherit all that money, man."

"Who cares about the fucking money, man?" Simon said. "I'd rather be on the streets than accept any of it if it makes me the kind of people my parents are: looking down on people, never coming home at night, always in the office. I don't want nothing to do with it. Least your mom wants you. Only time anyone's ever been nice to me is 'cause they thought I had money."

"Nah, man. I'm not like that. I don't give a fuck about your money."

Dio thought a while. Maybe Simon didn't have it made after all, always having people like him just for what he had. Dio knew what it was like to have nice things. Drug money did good things for him and his family, but he couldn't help but resent all the moochers who would come around whenever he had it. It never felt real. The only people who always treated him the same were Jennifer, his little brother, and, of course, Spooky, who had more money than he did.

It didn't make sense, any of it. Why was somebody like Simon in camp? What could he possibly have done?

"Hey, man, look!" Grossaint said, showing Franklin and his boys a letter. Coffee was curled up right next to him.

Dio rolled his eyes at them. He wondered what they were getting so excited about.

"Mike found my sisters, Joy and Rachel! Haven't found Terry yet, but . . ." Grossaint said, probably the happiest Dio had ever seen him.

"Really?" Franklin said.

"Yeah, man. Soon as I get out of here we're all getting together."

"Dude, that's great," Franklin said sadly. "You're lucky. I'm happy for you."

Then he started crying, actually crying. Dio wondered why. He never had taken the time to get to know Franklin.

Why would he? Franklin wanted nothing to do with him. All he could piece together from bits and pieces of conversations he had overheard was that somehow Franklin's only brother had been killed when his father beat him to a pulp in some drugged-up rage.

"'Snot right what parents do to kids," Grossaint said. "And the government don't do nothing about it. They break up perfectly good families just 'cause their parents might do a little drinking, just 'cause they might be a little poor. They'd never do it to some rich family."

This was a whole other side of Grossaint that Dio hadn't seen before—feelings, compassion. He actually cared about people. Dio often wondered whether, if he were white or if Grossaint were Mexican, maybe they could have been friends.

Franklin started bawling like crazy.

"It's all right, dude. You're all right, man," Grossaint said, soothing his friend. "Listen, you can look me up any time once we get out, you hear? Any time. I want you to meet everyone."

Grossaint noticed Dio staring and glared at him.

"You get all that work done?" Jackson asked Dio.

"Sir, yes, sir. Just have to finish one more bag of laundry."

"Good. Good. How's that girl of yours doing?"

"Sir, she's all right, sir," Dio answered. "A little down 'cause of all the medications and things."

"Yeah, that'll do that to ya."

Dio sensed that something was bothering Jackson and he just didn't seem to know how to say it.

"Whatcha going to do when you get out?" Jackson asked.

"Sir, get a job, I guess, sir. Provide for *mi amor*."

"That's good. What kind of job you thinking about?"

"Sir, not really sure, sir. Anything, to start. Been talking to Louise about doing something with art."

"Art? You can make a living doing art?"

"Sir, don't know, sir. Just a thought, sir."

"Well, if you're going to be an artist . . ."

Here come the lectures.

Dio felt like rolling his eyes. Jackson always tried to give advice; he just never was any good at it.

"You want to make sure you got something tangible behind you if you wanna provide for that girl of yours. You make sure you spend enough time with her. Women need that sort of thing. Just make sure you hold her, and you tell her you love her every day. They start to circumlocute if you don't do those sorts of things. What is *circumlocute*, trainee?"

"Sir, like, go away, stray, take off, or something like that, sir?"

"That's correct."

"Sir, is that what happened with you, sir? Did your wife—?"

"My wife? Which one?" He laughed. "Now, this has nothing to do with me. I'm just telling you from . . . I've seen these things happen. You hear?"

"Sir, yes, sir."

God, he wished he could get out of there.

This lecture was going to go on forever.

"Now if that's your dream to go and be an artist, you ought to go for it. That's your dream; you go on for it and don't let nobody stop you. Just make sure you get an education behind you. That's all I say. Tried to tell my son that."

"Sir, your son, sir?"

"Yep."

"Sir, did he listen, sir?"

"Well, started to. But sometimes things don't work out exactly how we want them to."

"Sir, yes, sir."

"He always was a hardheaded boy. Always had his head in the clouds. I guess if that makes ya happy, nothing wrong with that. Only get one chance at this life; might as well live the life we want."

"Sir, yes, sir. What's he do now, sir?

"He don't do nothing. He's dead."

Dio felt like a semi had hit him. He had had no idea.

"Sir, why's he . . . ? How'd he die, sir?"

"He . . . ain't none of your business. You just get on doing what you were doing."

"Sir, yes, sir."

Dio watched Jackson make his way out of the laundry room. He always seemed like such a confident man, but watching him there . . . he seemed like a man lost and alone.

Dio wondered what Senior Jackson did at night. *Who did he go home to? What was he like after work? Did he have a lady or was he stuck home alone most nights watching TV and eating Chinese food?*

Dio hated the thought of that. He hated thinking that could end up happening to him one day. He hated being alone, always had.

It was kind of strange: A few months ago Dio couldn't stand anybody at the camp, and now everyone was like his family. Louise was like his mother or aunt or something. Simon was like his little brother, and the rest of the guys at the camp were like cousins. Even Senior Jackson was kind of like his father.

Dio thought about the promise he had made to Louise. Giving his mother another chance seemed to be stupid. He loved his mom. There was no doubt about that, but she had done so many hateful, awful things to him as a kid, and he didn't know how to forgive her anymore.

~

Grossaint looked like he was going to cry. Everyone did, really, as the entire squad stood in front of the main gate looking at Coffee's dead body. Somehow she had gotten out and been hit by a car.

Dio hated that bratty little dog, but part of him loved her, too. It was sad, real sad.

"Well, we ought to get it off the road," Jackson said.

"Sir, Trainee Grossaint requests permission to speak, sir."

"Go ahead."

"Sir, how'd she get out, sir? We double-lock the gates all the time."

"Well, somebody was careless, that's for sure. Sometimes things happen, Grossaint. Things happen. Come on, now; help me. Simon, Franklin, let's go."

They all put on latex gloves and lifted her. Grossaint looked numb.

"Sorry about Coffee," Franklin said.

"Shit happens," Simon said. "Sometimes, shit happens."

Grossaint looked at him suspiciously.

"Right, Grossaint?" he added.

Dear Dio,

Thank you so much for your letter and the flowers you had sent from Vegas Flower Express. How'd you pull that off? It really lifted my spirits so much. It meant the world to me. You always know what to say to cheer me up. And you speak from the heart. It really shows in your writing.

Dio smelled the letter; it radiated her scent. He held it close, like it was her that he was holding, as he hid under his blanket, reading it with his flashlight.

Sorry I took so long to write back but a lots been going on here. Just know that I believe in you too Dio.

I know something good's going to happen to us.

I am feeling a lot better now. I'm still gaining weight but I've actually been outside. Angel took me out to a park and I needed it so bad. I felt so free. He even talked to my mom who's been a total worry wart and told her how important it is for me to get out and start living a normal life again. Somebody needed to talk to her. Thank God he did.

So I went to the park and I just sat by the pond and I didn't care about all the annoying gnats and things. I just breathed in the air and I felt the sunshine on me and it was just magical. I felt alive again. Angel even talked me into playing a little bit of guitar.

Music I need music it's like air to me. It like replenishes my soul when I sing. It's like God's gift to me. That's what I keep thinking of it as, Angel says, "God's gift and I have to give it back to the world."

Next week I'm going to start going to school again. It's going to be so weird. I know people are going talk about me behind my back but I don't care anymore. I'm just going to focus on my school work and come right home and I'm not going to get caught up in all that popularity crap. I am so over that.

Oh and I just wanted to let you know that Daniel's doing really well. He comes to our house just about every day after school and my mom makes him sit down and do his tarea. He's actually been getting A's Dio. Lots of them. You'd be so proud. And he's proud I can tell. He even acts all mamon when Desiree doesn't do well and says "No estupido you should do it this way or that way." You know it's really cute to see them together. They're actually best friends. Just like me and you were back when we were in junior high. It's almost like deja vu.

And I know you don't really want to talk about your mother but let me just say that Daniel says she's been really good. She hasn't been tomando at all and she came over the house the other day. She was a little shy and embarrassed. It was the first time she and my mom had spoken since everything happened. And she looked so much better Dio. She's really coming along.

I'm not going to nag you. It's just I don't understand why you can't forgive her. Perdonale. She's trying to change. And I can see it in her eyes Dio. She misses you and she feels hurt that you won't have anything to do with her. It hurt me to hear that you actually threw her letter away that she wrote you. You should give her another chance. She really loves you. Just think about it. OK?

So anyway, tell me about camp. What do you do all day anyway?

Love,
Jennifer

Dear Jennifer,

Damn girl. Took you forever to write back. Hey before I forget, Happy Birthday, I know your birthday's coming up soon. I can't exactly go out and buy you anything while I'm here but just know that I'm there with you in spirit. And no problem about the cheering you up. That's what I'm hear for, right?

Daniel's getting A's? You've got to be joking. I just want him to grow up and do much better than I did. He's real listo. I think he's smarter than me and he doesn't have to worry about some learning disability or nothing. That's what they say I have, A.D.D. But Daniel could be like a doctor or a lawyer or something big like that. Maybe even a corporate executive, who knows? The sky's the limit for that foo'.

Glad your going to school again. It's your senior year right? So you'll probably be graduating about the same time as me from boot camp.

I wish you would drop the whole subject about my mom. I'm tired of talking about it and I made up my mind already. She should have thought about that shit before she pulled it. What kind of mother tells you from the time you're a chavalillo that you're a loser that you'll never be nothing but a bum on the street when you're only 13? What kind of mom beats up on you and slaps the shit out of you and knows you can't do nothing about it to fight back. I'll tell you, if she were a dude I would have kicked her ass a long time ago.

Louise says I've got a lot of anger in me. No shit. Tengo razones. But every time I get encabronado about something I'm learning to just work it out. You know. I let off the steam whenever they make us do burpies and shit. You know what Jennifer? I can do 100 pushups without stopping. Not girl pushups either. When I got here I could do like 2. But Sr. Jackson just pushes us and there were times when I thought there was no way in hell I could do any more but he always says, "90% mental, 10% physical." I think it's true. I think there's lots of stuff people think they can't do and they can't only cause they think they can't.

I'm learning a lot here. You'd be proud of me. I'm working hard. And I don't want to sound like I love this place or anything. I'll be the first mutha fucka out the door when I graduate, believe me. But I'm just saying some of the people out here aren't as bad as I thought they were at first.

Only person who hasn't changed is Grossaint. He's this Nazi motherfucker. He's nuts. I mean I really think he might be crazy.

Louise says that everything happens for the greater good. Do you think that's true? Looking back, maybe it is true. I like who I'm becoming Jennifer. Me caigo bien. And now I see like there are a lot of different opportunities out there for me if I work really hard.

See here's how it works. Everyone starts out all wearing black, see? They just moved us up to stripes, last level is white. That means we're about ready to graduate.

Even Simon's changing. You ought to see him now. He got swoll. They ain't big muscles like mine or anything but at least he's got a little meat on his bones. He's like a little me. Doesn't put up with shit. I told him from the beginning, "They fuck with you, you gotta fuck 'em worse." It's true and he took it to heart.

I miss you baby.

Love,
Dio

PS: Who's this Angel dude you keep talking about? These foo's keep clownin' me saying he's your new sancho. But he's gay isn't he? I mean with a name like Angel? I told these babosos they're stupid. Besides I know you wouldn't do me like that. You know we're together forever. Just like you said, "True love lasts forever." Right?

Things were going really well for him that day. In fact, they had gone well for him most of the week. He was being given more and more responsibility and was even doing really well in school. Dio figured they were only about a couple of months away from the last level of boot camp, and he couldn't wait. Every day he was getting closer and closer to getting out, and he was really starting to take a good look at his life. He was thinking about some of the decisions he had made in the past. The things he was learning kept echoing in his mind over and over again.

Jackson never put up with any excuses, not from him, not from anybody. Dio knew he could no longer make any excuses for his decisions. He knew that just because he had grown up in a bad part of town, with a shitty mom and a terrible school system, it was no excuse for not picking himself up by his own bootstraps and making the best of it.

Jackson was proud of him; that was obvious. Oh, sure, he tried to hide it. He'd never been the type of guy to lavish compliments on people or to really show any type of affection, but Dio couldn't help but see through all that. He could see the twinkle in Jackson's eyes when Dio did well on the obstacle courses or when he led the squad in assignments. He could see the small smile he tried to hide whenever he heard Dio repeating something that he had taught him. Dio knew that he couldn't be more proud.

Jackson strolled through the grounds that day like he did every day around the same time to check on the different squads. The last level of squad, or what was left of them, were doing well, and he only hoped they'd continue on the right path once they got out. One thing he hated to think about was doing all this work he went through shaping these young men into something special, and then having all that work go to waste. He passed through the hooches, peered in at Dio's squad in the laundry room, then walked around the corner and found him—Grossaint.

At first he didn't think anything of it. Grossaint was just by the garbage with a couple of his trainee buddies and looked like he was just dumping trash. But then he heard that distinct sound, that sound Jackson knew only in memories, that sniffling, sucking-up-tears sound that guys made when they didn't want anyone to know they had been crying. Jackson squinted and zeroed in on his target. He marched toward Grossaint, who immediately stood at attention.

"Sir, by your leave, sir."

"No. Stay put."

Jackson examined him; his eyes were still puffy, his nose still running.

"What's wrong with you, Grossaint?"

"Sir, nothing, sir."

"Tell me."

"Sir, it's no big deal. It's just . . . Trainee Grossaint doesn't want to say, sir. He doesn't want to get him in trouble, sir," Grossaint said, hoping the onion he held tightly in his hand wouldn't be noticed. "He's Trainee Grossaint's friend."

Jackson moved into Grossaint's face and barked at him. "Don't want to get who in trouble? Tell me, Grossaint."

Dio smiled as he saw Jackson approach. He knew he'd be proud of all the work they had gotten done that day, and maybe he'd even let them off early.

Dio's body was sore. He'd been lifting bags and bags of laundry all day with Simon and the rest of the squad. And he'd welcome an early break. But then Dio's smile faded. Jackson was moving like a locomotive and he had Grossaint by the neck, leading him toward Dio. They were followed by two junior officers. Something was wrong, very wrong.

They halted in front of Dio.

"Sir, Trainee Rodríguez requests permission to—"

"Shut up, Radigez," he commanded. "Show me where it is, Grossaint."

He released Grossaint and went directly behind Dio, to where a giant washer was. He started pulling the washer back.

What is going on? Dio wondered.

And then he saw. There it was, clear as day, a giant hole in the wall directly behind the washer. Not the small hole that he had punched through, but instead a hole big enough to crawl out of, leading directly out of the gates that locked them in. His mouth dropped. And he knew exactly what it looked like.

"Sir, I—"

"Did you do this, Radigez? Did you?"

"Sir, Trainee Rodríguez . . . yes, but no, not—"

Simon tried to step up in front of Dio. "Sir, it wasn't his—"

"Shut up, Simon. Radigez, did you do this, or not?"

"Sir, no, sir. Not like that, sir."

Jackson stepped in front of Dio, nose to nose, and said in a low voice, "Now, I'm going to ask you again, did you do that?"

"Sir, I . . . I . . . sir, no, sir," Dio stuttered.

"Sir, yes he did, sir," Grossaint answered. "I saw him."

"Sir, so did Trainee Franklin, sir," Franklin added. One by one they all said, "Sir, so did I, sir."

Dio felt like his world was closing in on him.

"What's the tenth general rule, Radigez?"

"Sir, I had nothing to do with—"

"Shut up, Radigez. I don't talk to liars. Take him away."

The junior officers grabbed Dio and yanked him away.

"Sir, it wasn't me, sir! It wasn't me, sir!"

Jackson just shook his head in disbelief. "You give 'em an inch . . ." is all he said.

Dio's eyes met Simon's. He looked like a little lost puppy, with Grossaint and his boys circling him like vultures, ready to devour their prey.

As if a week in the hole weren't bad enough, what made it even worse was that when Dio did get out, they stripped him of his striped outfit and put him back in the dark clothes, the first level.

They took away most of his personal possessions and moved him into a tent with a beginner squad. Everyone stared at him. They knew what had happened.

And he'd come so close to graduating . . .

Dio didn't know how he'd be able to make it through everything all over again. He was no longer the leader of a group. He felt like sludge, like slop for pigs. He didn't feel like he was standing out anymore. He felt like he was barely alive. His eyes burned with the thought that he wouldn't be able to see Jennifer any time in the near future.

It was a hot summer day, burning outside, but Dio shivered. He felt cold inside, cold and alone, as he cradled himself in his bunk and sobbed. At first he sobbed as quietly as he could, but then he couldn't help himself; tears came out uncontrollably and so did his sobs.

He tried to ignore all the "Shut up!" comments from the new trainees. He felt powerless. He couldn't help it. He wished Jennifer were there; this time he wanted for her to hold him. He longed to hear her voice again, to see her, for her to encourage him and tell him that everything would be all right and that he'd make it through this.

He knew he hadn't done anything wrong, but he couldn't help but feel like a total failure. What kept haunting his mind was that somehow he wasn't being a good example for his brother, that even his brother would be ashamed of him. He had so many plans, so many things he wanted to do as soon as he got out, but now . . .

Dio worried about Simon. He wondered how Simon was ever going to be able to make it without him around, and he knew Grossaint would take advantage of the situation. Dio wouldn't be there to protect him. They would no doubt pick on him, tear him apart until he was completely defenseless, and they'd find joy in every moment of it.

He could feel the self-doubt coming over him like a dense fog, like poisonous black exhaust from an old pickup truck. Maybe they were right. Maybe he'd always be a loser. Maybe all his big dreams and plans would never come to pass. Maybe he'd never amount to anything.

To top it all off, it had been weeks since he had heard from Jennifer. He wondered what was so important that kept her from writing him back for so long. Didn't she know that he needed her? He resisted the urge to write her again. He didn't want to come across as desperate, but desperate was exactly how he felt. A letter from her was just the welcome mat he needed.

Didn't she remember all that he had done for her?

⸻

After Jennifer came to him with that black eye, he couldn't contain himself. He did stay with her that night, but the next day, after Spooky heard what happened, he riled Dio up, and before he knew it, his whole crew was tracking Wiggie down.

Wham! Dio slammed Wiggie against the restaurant window and started pounding him. He was a skinny, peckerwood white guy in his forties, with brown hair and now with a bloody mouth and nose.

His stooges—whom Dio called Acne, a guy in his twenties

covered with acne scars, and Dirty Blond, who looked like the worst kind of fat trailer trash—had their hands busy fighting off Spooky and Dio's homies.

Dio cocked his *cohete* in Wiggie's face. "You ever lay another hand on her and I'll kill ya. Ya hear?"

He shoved the gun in his temple again. "I said ya hear, fucking *puto*?"

"Yeah," he answered, with hate in his eyes. "Who your girl?"

"Jennifer, stupid."

"You mean Sunshine, that Latina cunt?"

Dio came at him again. "What the fuck did you say?"

Spooky spotted patrol cars approaching. "Dio, let's go."

But it was too late; Spooky and his boys had taken off, but the cops caught up to Dio. Even Acne, Wiggie, and Dirty Blond got away. Otherwise Dio would have finished them off. He knew his mom was going to be pissed; she had warned him that if he fucked up again she'd kick him out of the house. But she'd do the same thing if she were in the same situation. Wouldn't she? He knew it wasn't the wisest decision, but nobody hurt his lady, nobody.

＿゜＿

They didn't even let Dio work in the kitchen anymore. He hoped that someone told Louise what had happened so that she didn't think he just didn't show up. He wondered what she'd think and if she'd believe him when he told her he had nothing to do with the hole in the wall. He knew he was lucky, in a way, because anyone accused of trying to escape could have easily been sentenced to serve the rest of his term in real prison. But just the thought of starting all over again—Dio hated it.

Three days passed before Dio was able to see Louise. She'd been off for that long anyway, and still looked like she was suffering from a cold by the time he saw her serving chow. She motioned for him to go to the back of the kitchen and Dio slipped away, knowing he'd only have five minutes at the most before someone would notice he was gone.

"What happened?" she asked with urgency. "Did you do it? I told you to keep your nose clean."

"I didn't do nothing," Dio said. "You got to believe me."

"I know," she said softly.

"He set me up for this, I know."

"Who?"

"Grossaint."

"How do you know?"

"Who else would do this? I swear to God, I'm going to get him. I'm going to beat his—"

"Listen to me," she said, checking to see if anyone was listening. "That's the kind of attitude that got you into this place and it's the kind of attitude that will get you in prison if you keep it up."

"What do you want me to do?"

"Walk away from it."

"You crazy? You don't know what it's like. I've been putting up with these fucking peckerwoods my whole life. They're always stabbing you in the back."

"Not all white people are like that, Dio."

"Yeah? Yeah? Do you know what it's like every time you walk down the street to have people in every car that pulls up next to you lock their doors? You know what it's like to have people ask you if you speak English just 'cause you're brown? You know what it's like to be pulled up to some strange man's house with your friends and . . ."

Dio fought the tears.

"And what, Dio?"

"We were just using the pay phone outside, me and my homies Spider, Bullet, and Trix. We all grew up together, knew each other since we was like five. We were just outside of Spooky's girl's apartment, minding our business. And some fucking big white guy grabbed us all by the neck and forced us into his apartment. We didn't know what to do. We were only thirteen years old and we were scared to death. Come to find out, he was the manager of the apartment, and someone called saying four Mexicans were checking people's doors to see if they were open. He assumed it was us; called the cops and everything. They smacked us around, called us fucking spics, used their fucking sticks on us and everything, 'cause they said we were mouthing off. But we didn't do nothing, Louise, nothing. We were just using the phone, didn't say anything to anyone. But who would have believed us, four Mexicans dressed like thugs. That kind of shit happened to me every day."

"Rise above it, Dio. You gotta show Grossaint, you got to show them all, nothing's going to get to you. You gotta walk away and become something when you graduate. Listen to me, success is the greatest revenge."

Dio felt his eyes and nose sting again. He wasn't going to cry, not this time, but he was burning up inside. He felt like punching something, anything. He slammed his fist against the doorframe.

"I swear to God, Louise. I'm going to go crazy in here."

"You got to make it, Dio. I know. I know it's hard. But you got to. Think about Jennifer. Just keep thinking about being with her. You want to be with her, don't you?"

Dio sighed.

"Well, don't you?"

"Of course. She don't even write me no more."

"She will, Dio. She will. You know she will. Now focus on that." Her eyes shifted, spotting someone in the distance. "Get back before they notice."

Dio started back. Then it occurred to him, "What happened with your date? Your soul mate?"

Her eyes met the floor. "We'll talk about that later. Get going."

It couldn't be good, Dio knew, not with a reaction like that. It seemed like everyone had their share of problems. He hoped for a miracle, anything that would help him through.

If Dio thought he had it bad, it was nothing compared with what Simon was going through. Simon felt just as alone, for one thing. It seemed like all the people that were on his side before, when Dio was there, had scattered as soon as he was taken away.

Simon hadn't been himself ever since the whole thing happened. He'd disappear for hours and come back in a daze. Even Jackson was starting to notice and had him sent to the nurse, but they couldn't find anything wrong. The other train-ees thought he must have been losing his mind. Simon would just say he was fine.

But he wasn't fine. Something was definitely wrong. Something was eating at him, and losing his head was the one relief Simon could rely on. He felt like he was a skeleton, without flesh. He could see Grossaint's prying eyes on him, like a dog ready to gnaw on his bone. And Grossaint didn't waste any time, either.

"Hey, darky!" Grossaint said, bumping into Simon as he carried a pail of dirty bleach water down the hall of the main building. It slopped all over the floor.

"Dirty nigger," he said, leaving everyone laughing at him. "Why don't you go pick it up, Simon? Huh? Pick it up and be a good little boy for us."

Simon's rage built inside him. He started for Grossaint, only to fall on his ass as he slipped on the suds. They roared with laughter. Grossaint towered over him.

"Who the fuck do you think you are, coon? Your dirty wetback's not here to help you. Shit happens, Simon. Some-times shit happens. Now whatcha gonna do? Huh? Huh?" he screamed in Simon's face as he kicked him in the side.

His boys each gave Simon a kick in the side as Simon

gasped for air, looking at all the trainees just watching in shock, but doing nothing.

"Help," he muttered.

He wanted to call out louder, but he couldn't muster the strength. At the same time, he didn't dare say anything, because God only knew what Grossaint might do that was even worse.

Dear Dio,

Thanks yeah. Had a great birthday. Sorry I'm taking so long to write. Things are really kicking in with school. I've got so much to catch up on but the teachers have been really nice. And Angel and my friends have been helping me with the homework and things. And before you get any thoughts in your mind, Angel's just my friend. Just my social worker, that's it. He's just been really nice to me and really worked hard to get things going in my life. It's part of his job. It's nothing for you to be concerned about.

Anyway, I'm glad to hear you got your stripes and that you're making progress. Won't be long before you're out of there, right? I bet you can't wait. And I'm glad you're making a lot more friends. Tell Simon and them I said HI.

Oh and speaking of friends, I've met some homegirls at school that I'm starting to hang out with again. My mom is acting so ob-noxious though. She makes me come home by 8 o'clock like I'm in the 6th grade or something. I was just like 15 minutes late the other night y ya mero se cagaba en sus pantalones.

Anyway, guess what? I started taking jazz class again. I got my cast off last week and I'm taking it really easy, really slow but everyone thought it'd be a good idea. Except my mom of course.

She's such a worrywart. That's all she does is chipiliar me; and it's driving me crazy but I'm trying my best just to think positive. And like Angel says, I've got to think about why she's doing it. She cares about me. I just wish she'd care about me a little bit less sometimes.

I've even been looking in CallBack Magazine for auditions. I might start going to them, not right away but it just gets me pumped up again. I think I can really land something Dio I really do.

I'm mostly pretty much back to myself. Sometimes I've been a little dizzy and I've been getting the flu a lot lately. I mean just throwing up and everything and it can't be the medication cause I'm done with it. So Angel's going to take me to the doctor's office tomorrow morning to see what might be going on. I hope they don't give me more medication. I can't stand that stuff.

Oh and I almost forgot to tell you about the "romance saga" between Daniel and Desiree. Well they were all loving each other and everything. Holding hands, you know how 4th graders are. And my mom had signed them up for this little league type of thing. It's starts in the spring and goes all through the fall. Well anyway, they're play-ing softball all right. And I don't know what happened exactly cause I was talking to Angel about something but all I know is that Des-iree's laughing at Daniel cause he's been striking out and the next thing I know Desiree's on the ground llorando and Daniel's saying "It's not my fault. It's not my fault. I'm sorry. I'm sorry."

So somehow he says, he threw the bat back behind him when he was walking off the field and it hit her in her cara. We had to take her to the hospital and they put a few stitches on her fore-head. She's been pissed at him ever since and he's been trying to make it up to her. She won't let it go. Desiree will get over it though. I know her.

Mom's practically adopted Daniel into the family. And your mom and my mom have been actually having coffee and things at the house. It's kind of weird. I think they're actually becoming friends. Imagine that.

Thanks for being such a good friend Dio. You've always been there for me and I'll always appreciate it.

Anyway, I'm so glad things are going so great for you. You deserve it. What do you do all day?

Your Best Friend,
Jennifer

What does he do all day? Dio wanted to say, "Nothing but think about you," because he didn't want her to know about all the drama that had been happening. She sounded so proud of him, with all the changes he was making, and now he couldn't bear to tell her. He knew he could tell Jennifer anything, but things were different now.

If she found out that he had gotten in trouble again, she'd think he was just the thug he was when he started this camp—but he was so much more than that. Besides, he didn't want to bring her down. It seemed like things were going so much better for her now.

What was he going to do? Tell her how he was knocked back to the first level? Tell her how he just wanted to die? How he wondered if he'd even make it through? How awful it was to see Grossaint taking over the responsibilities he once had and enjoying every moment of it? How he wanted to crack Grossaint's skull open?

He could never say any of those things to her, not now.

Not when he was so close to winning her back. But how would he explain the delay? She was expecting him to be released in a few months. Dio didn't know what to do, but he couldn't spill the beans. That he knew for sure.

But Jennifer had what Dio called "woman's intuition"; she knew things. He didn't know how she knew things, but she could read him like a book. He just hoped she wouldn't pick up on anything.

Dear Jennifer,

I'm glad things are going well for you. And I'm glad you're keeping busy. Things for me are going real ~~good~~ *well. I'm making strides in the squad and everyone's really liking me. Even Sr. Jackson says he's real proud of me and if I keep working real hard then he thinks I can accomplish anything.*

Dio hated lying to her, but what else was he supposed to do?

I hope that Desiree's OK. Tell Daniel I said to watch it and keep his temper. It's stuff like that that gets you in a place like this. I miss him Mija. And I miss you. I can't wait to see you and I think about you every night still. I know you're busy but don't get too busy for me. We're connected, that's what Louise tells me. She thinks you and I are soul mates and so do I. We'll always be connected.

I think about what life's going to be like and I've got all these plans for us. We're going to travel the country. ~~Infact~~ *In fact, we're going to travel the world Jennifer. We're going to see places you've* only dreamed of and you know what? I'm even going to go to college. I am. I know it's strange to hear me say that. Isn't it baby? But I've been doing real ~~good~~ well lately and Sr. Jackson keeps telling me to go for my dreams but have a solid foundation. Truth is I've always thought about college. I just didn't think I could ever go. But they say you can get grants and things to pay for it and I'm keeping my grades up.

Life is good, but it would be better with you by my side. I love you baby. You're my girl, you're my everything. Remember Visitor's Day is coming up next week so I hope you can take an hour out of your busy schedule and see me.

Love,
Your Soul Mate,
Dio

Dio thought for a while. There was something in her letter that bothered him. It wasn't that she was spending so much time with that Angel guy; for all he knew, he was gay. It was just that she called Dio her "friend." It just didn't feel right. It felt condescending. It felt distant. It felt cold. It made Dio feel like he was being detached from her and he didn't like it one bit. But he didn't say anything. Why ruin a good thing?

Once again Dio stood in line alone as he watched the room full of visitors busy with activity. Everyone seemed so happy, but he hated it. He was embarrassed and hurt. Jennifer once again hadn't shown up, and he was beginning to feel a burning rage at her that he never had felt before.

He let his mind trail off as he watched a trainee with what looked like his girlfriend. They looked so much in love. He could tell by the way they were touching each other's hands. He could feel it. They kissed, then kissed again, and before long were full-out making out. One of the officers had to break it up. Dio smirked.

He missed that with Jennifer. He missed the silly things they did together and just sitting next to her and not talking. They didn't have to talk; they could just be together and that was enough.

They'd park way east in Las Vegas, almost against the mountains—hills really. They could see the whole city. It was so quiet, so gorgeous during the day, but at night, when the moon was humongous like a giant spotlight, it was breathtaking.

They'd sit atop the hood of his Chevy, just him and Jennifer. He loved moments like that. He'd slide his hand across the hood, his hand joining hers, and they'd kiss. Her lips always tasted like cherry, his favorite flavor.

He would just watch her, as minutes passed, while the wind danced with her hair. She'd smile at him adoringly and ask why he was staring and he'd say simply, "'Cause you're so beautiful."

Dio smiled at the thought.

"Sorry I'm late."

Dio turned to see his mother, of all people in the world, standing in front of him. It was like waking up from a dream, a really good dream, to find that you were still stuck in the shitty life you lived.

She looked a mess. Not a drunken mess, like usual, but the wind had messed up her hair and her makeup was all over the place. Too much blue eye shadow—that was his mom's trademark. She kept trying to reposition her big-assed purse and she looked nervous as hell.

"Do we have any time?"

"A little," Dio said.

"Good." She smiled nervously. "I found out from the court you had Visitor's Days every month. Why didn't you tell me? Let's sit down."

He swallowed. He didn't know if he should be glad to see her, to see anyone, really, or if he should feel what he felt inside, which was hard to explain—anger, but obligation. Dio had been so angry with her for so long. At the same time, he missed his mommy. He missed her smile, her laughter; he missed the way things were before his dad died.

They sat on a bench, as far apart as he could manage. It seemed that all of the noise in the room suddenly disappeared. It was just him and her.

"Still saying your prayers?" she asked.

"Yep."

"Good. You look good," she said, reaching for his face. But when he turned away, her smile faded from embarrassment and hurt. She cleared her throat.

"Did you get my letter?"

He nodded.

"You read it?"

He sighed. "Haven't got to it yet."

"Haven't got to it? Dio, it's been months." She tried to work up a smile. "Your birthday's coming up soon, isn't it?"

"Is this going to take long?" Dio asked.

"Now, is that any way to talk to your mother? I came here to see you."

"It's been almost a year. Why start now? Why start caring now?"

"Now, that's not nice. You know I care. Don't say I don't care, *mijo*."

"Don't call me that. Don't call me *mijo*."

She looked around to make sure no one was listening, like she always did. She regrouped for a second. "I'm in A.A. now," she said sheepishly. "Things are different now. I've been sober for—"

"Again?"

"I'm going to make it this time, *mi*—Dio. I know it. It's been four months. I got a job working in a office. Can you believe it? Me? A office?" She laughed, hoping he'd laugh with her, but he just stared at her instead.

"An."

"What?"

"An office," Dio said. "You're working at an office."

She laughed nervously. "Well, excuse the hell out of me. What are you, some spelling expert now? . . . So . . . you're doing good in school, then. I'm proud of you."

"Well. The word is well. I'm doing well in school," he said, cool as ice.

He knew she wanted him to rejoice with her. And part of him wanted to really badly, too. He wanted to share with his mother her joy, how proud of her he was, but he couldn't help but wonder how long it would last. After all, this wasn't the first time she'd claimed to be sober. But it was the longest period of time she'd stayed sober. He just didn't want to be disappointed with her again.

He wanted to put his arms around her and hug her tight. He wanted to embrace her and never let her go. He wanted to cry because he was so happy for her. He wanted to share with her all the joys and the pains and the changes he'd made inside boot camp. He'd always wanted a mother he could tell everything to, but he never had that and he just couldn't start now. He didn't know what it was. Was it because he couldn't trust her? Was it because he couldn't let all the pain she'd caused in the past go? He wanted to connect with her. He wanted to tell her everything, but something always held him back.

She tried to laugh his comments off, but he could tell they bothered her.

"Well, I'm glad you're doing well in school then. And you're behaving yourself?"

He rolled his eyes. "Sure."

"Good. Good. Oh, Daniel's doing so good, so well in school now, too."

"I know."

"He's got a little girlfriend now."

"I know."

"What do you mean you know? How do you know?"

"Jennifer told me."

She looked like she had seen a ghost. "J-j-j-jennifer? She? You still? How do you talk to her?"

"She writes me letters. She didn't tell you?"

"No, I had no— Well, I'm glad. I'm glad you're still friends."

"We're more than just friends, Mom. We're a couple."

She looked down at her feet. "Are you? How do you know? I mean, it's been so long."

"What do you mean how do I know? It could be fifty years and she'd wait for me."

She just looked at him for a while. "Maybe . . . Jennifer's a pretty girl, Dio—"

"I know."

"And you're a good-looking guy. You know that."

"What are you saying?"

"You're both so young. She's got—you've both got lots of choices. Both of you."

"We've already made our choice. Jennifer said she and I are forever. We made a promise to each other."

She seemed to want to tell Dio something, but she couldn't, and he couldn't bear to think of what it might be.

"You got something to say, just say it," he said.

She just tried to work up a smile. "You look so good now," was all she could get out.

"I don't want anyone else, Mom. . . . You're just jealous."

"Jealous?" She laughed.

"Yeah, jealous 'cause I found someone that wants me

and wants me forever. I'm not going through women like you've gone through men."

"Now, that's not fair. That's not fair, *mijo*. You make it sound like I'm some kind of . . . slut," she whispered, once again making sure no one heard her. "I'm not. I haven't always had the best taste in men, but I wasn't always . . . well, I couldn't always see all that in front of me with all the drinking and the partying and the—"

"There are no excuses in the world, Mom. You blame everyone but yourself. You did this. You made your life that way. Nobody else."

"I know. I know that, *mijo*."

"I told you, don't call me that. I'm not your son. You think you had it hard. How do you think I felt growing up with a drunk? How do you think I felt being beat up all the time?"

"I'm sorry about that. You know I'm sorry about that. I've said I'm sorry."

"You gave me up when I was thirteen," Dio said. "You abandoned me. You let me go from house to house, from foster home to foster home. Daniel even forgot who I was by the time I came back. You could have bailed me out before I came here. You knew I was innocent, but you let them take me away."

"I didn't. I didn't know . . . you were innocent. I said I'm sorry. I've said it a thousand times. You've kicked me while I'm down. Now, what else do you want me to do? I'm sorry, okay. I'm sorry!"

"Well, I don't believe you," Dio answered back.

She was trembling by now. She got up to leave, turned to say something, but could only point her finger at him.

"*Que descanse en paz*, what would your father think? You . . . you . . . sometimes I wish I never had you."

His eyes started to sting. He wasn't going to cry, wasn't going to give her the pleasure. He watched her walk away, fading out of the room, a hurt soul. He knew he'd hurt her badly; he'd gotten her back for the pain she had caused, but somehow it didn't do anything for him. It didn't give him the pleasure he thought it might.

Thinking back on it, he wished he'd never said those things. He only wanted to let her know how he felt, but it hadn't come out the way he had wanted. He wiped his tears before anyone saw them.

Chapter Six

$\mathcal{I}$T HAD BEEN A WHOLE MONTH. HIS BIRTHDAY CAME AND went, but still no word from Jennifer. Every day had been a living hell for Dio. He was doing all the chores and things that the beginning squad had to do. He was still going to school; that was the only time he ever saw his old squad in passing. But Jackson never let him talk to them. Dio felt awful. He knew he was innocent. He never would have been so stupid as to try to escape, but still, somehow he felt like he had let Jackson down. He missed things the way they used to be. He and Jackson were starting to really bond. He was even starting to like Jackson, surprisingly enough, but now he felt every time he was around him, Jackson wanted nothing to do with him. Jackson kept his distance. He was cold, with no feeling in his voice. He acted like Dio was just prisoner number 28310, and that was it.

But Dio's mind was racing. He had nothing else to do but think about Jennifer, no friends to talk to anymore, so his whole world revolved around thinking about her. His imagination tossed and turned with ideas about her and Angel together. He felt her distance and something told him that she wasn't telling him everything that was going on there. He didn't understand how someone could be that cold, how someone he shared such a special connection with could just not contact him. He was tired of hearing Louise tell him to give her the benefit of the doubt, because he had done that already, time and time again. Something was going on, something she didn't want him to know about, something she wasn't telling him.

Dear Jennifer,

Why's it taking you so long to write me back? And what did you mean in your last letter calling me your "friend"? You act like we're not going out anymore or something.

I don't like the idea of you spending so much time with this joto Angel. And you didn't answer my question. He is a joto. Isn't he? I just don't like it. Don't you have any of your homegirls to hang out with instead?

You shouldn't take that long to write back. How long does it take to drop a letter. No more than a hour. That's it. That's how long it takes me and that's including stuffing it in the envelope and dropping it off in the mail box, and I know it's a lot easier for you than me.

Damn girl, you need to stop thinking about yourself. I told you how important your letters are to me. You don't know how hard it is here. You know I love you. I need you baby and I need you by my side.

I'm sorry if I sound pissed it's just all the homeboys think you're going out with that Angel guy and it's not making me look good. I told them all these great things about you and it's starting to make me have doubts.

I know you got all that shit going on but you can't be that ocupada. You don't know the meaning of busy Jennifer. We get up at 5 o'clock every morning and we're doing a mile run, push-ups, chinups, situps, burpies, and breakfast before you even crawl out of bed. Then we go work detail and cleaning and more pushups, chinups, and everything after that we do all that kind of shit until it's like 8 o'clock on top of school and everything else and I still make time to write you. So I know you ain't that busy.

Anyway baby, Visitor's Day's coming up again in a few weeks soon so please make it this time. I wish I could be there for you on Cinco De Mayo like last year. But just know I'd be there if I could. I need to see you or I'm going to go loco, 'K?

Love
Dio

"I've got only fifteen minutes," Dio told Louise.

She took him into the pantry where they could talk in private.

His junior officer had asked him to carry some supplies into the kitchen and he knew he could have only a few good quality minutes with Louise before the officer would start looking for him.

"How you holding up?" she asked.

"Don't worry about me. What's going on with you? What happened with the soul-mate guy?"

She started rearranging things on the shelf like she always did when she got nervous.

"Well?" he insisted.

"Memories are funny things, Dio. Sometimes our imagination fills in the blanks. Things aren't always as good as we thought they were. Anyways, my husband called again. Wants to go out on a date," she said, rolling her eyes and trying to hide her smile.

"You're going to get back together with that *puto*? You sure?"

"He's changing. Trying to change, anyway. It's worth a shot. Even you said God doesn't like divorce. We'll see how it goes."

"He hurts you again, you just let me know," Dio said seriously.

She laughed.

"I know, I know. Have you heard from Jennifer lately?"

"She's still playing her games."

"I'm sorry to hear that, Dio. But maybe—"

"Maybe nothing. It takes only a few minutes to write a letter. She just doesn't want to."

"You really think that?"

"Yeah."

She sat on the countertop and patted a place for Dio, too.

"How are you feeling?" she asked.

"How do you think I'm feeling?"

"That bad?"

He nodded. She struggled with something encouraging to say, but, not being able to think of anything, she just sat with him.

"Things will turn around," she finally said.

"How do you know?"

"'Cause . . . 'cause if there's one thing I know, Dio, it's that this too shall pass. My mother once said to me that if you catch a bird and let it go, it'll go; if it's meant to come back to you, it will."

"That makes a hell of a lot of sense," Dio snapped sarcastically.

"Just give it some thought."

But Dio didn't even want to entertain the thought. Letting her go was out of the question. He couldn't even fathom the thought of living his life without her. She was his everything.

"How are your grades doing?"

"All right."

"Not that good, huh?"

"Not really."

"Know what you need to do, Dio? You've got to get rid of all this anger inside you. As soon as you get back to the hooch, I want you to write a letter to Jennifer, write a letter to your mom, write a letter to anyone and pour your heart and soul into it. I mean, I want you to just say what you've always wanted to say, just let it all out. That's what I do. It works, I'm telling you. Even put it in an envelope and seal it up. I mean don't send it or anything but you'll be amazed how much tension that releases."

Dio sighed; he was tired of all these psychobabble tips. He just wanted Jennifer back. Couldn't she see that?

"Dio, concentrate on your schoolwork right now. I know it's hard, but try. Jennifer will be there for you one way or another. You'll see. You've got to be the man she's looking for when you get out, right?"

He nodded. Her advice just went in one ear and out the other. His mind was adrift, thinking about Jennifer. He didn't want to hear about schoolwork. He didn't want to hear about later. He didn't want to hear about maybe. He only wanted to hear Jennifer's soft voice. He wanted to experience how great it felt for her to whisper in his ear, or to smell the scent of her neck and ears as he nibbled on them. He only wanted to hold her and love her, but the frustration of weeks without hearing from her was getting to him and he couldn't understand the disrespect she was showing for him.

⌒

As soon as Dio got back to the hooch, he grabbed paper and pen. What could be the harm in trying out Louise's advice? Why not just write it all out? Jennifer would never see it anyway. Once he started writing, he couldn't stop. He even took the letter with him to his work detail.

Dear Jennifer,
    Why you ignoring my letters? No entiendo. It's like all this stuff I say from my heart don't mean shit to you. What's up with you? Why you changed? You not the sweet girl I knew.

But maybe I didn't know you were a skank like I thought I did before. You a slut, you'll always be a slut and I know you're out there putiando.

You ain't even patient. You probably had a sancho on the side when we were going out. You probably trickin' with Wiggie again. That's probably what's keeping you so busy.

I don't want your fucking pussy no more anyway. It's all stank and you probably got some nasty disease anyway, I wouldn't want my cock up in it anyway. It's like a community bathroom or something. That's what it's like.

You just cold. You don't treat me the way I should be treated at all. You act like all the times we been together don't mean nothing to you at all.

I'm sorry I ever met you. I'm sorry I put my heart and soul in you. I'm sorry I've wasted all this time dreaming we'd ever be anymore than fuck buds. And we weren't even that.

I can get any bitch I want to. You don't know what you got. I could pick up any hoe on the street. Got you didn't I? You'd do anything for 20 bills. That's what you did. You played me. You played my feelings.

How could you treat me like that? How could you do me like that. You as cold as a snake. And you going to get what you deserve when I get out. You going to be sorry you ever played me like you did.

Te voy a dar en tu pinche madre! You a bitch. You a hoe. You a slut. I hope you die out there in the streets. I hope your moms and pops kick your ass out again.

Nobody wants a puta for a daughter and that what you is. You know it too. You talk about all these bullshit dreams. They

ain't never going to happen for you anyway unless you fuck your
way to the top. And that's probably what you'll try to do.

But once they find out you ain't nothing but a street hooker
they'll drop your ass like I'm going to drop your ass.

Fuck you Jennifer. Fuck you.

Dio Playboy

Dio couldn't write fast enough. He was crouched in a corner of the main building, stealing away a few minutes to write. No one was around and even if they were he wouldn't have noticed them.

He was so pent up inside he felt like he had to get it out. He sealed the envelope, put Jennifer's address, even put a stamp on it. Maybe he should just mail it, let her know how he was feeling, but he couldn't let it go. He couldn't drop it in the mail drop. Something was stopping him. More than anything, he was scared. He was scared of losing Jennifer. He knew if he sent that letter that would be it. He'd never see her again and their years together, all those years of struggling and loving each other, would be gone and he'd never be able to take it back. He knew if he sent it, he'd regret it.

Worse yet, without Simon around, without Jennifer, he'd have no one. He'd be alone. Sure, there were his homies back in Vegas, but still nothing was the same; nothing was like losing your lady.

"What are you doing?"

Dio jumped up. His heart jumped with him as he stood at attention, Jackson in front of him.

"Ssss-sir. I . . . I was just . . ."

"Mmm-hmm. I bet. You get all your work done?"

"Sir, yes, sir!"

"You keeping your nose clean?"

"Sir, yes, sir."

"And your grades?"

"Sir, getting better, sir."

"Good, 'cause we don't let no dullards graduate. What's a *dullard*, trainee?"

"Sir, a dummy, sir."

Jackson smiled. "Good . . . good."

Dio's eyes followed Jackson as he paced back and forth, walking around him, examining him.

"How you making out?"

"Sir, all right, sir. Trainee Rodríguez is managing."

"And your girl?"

Dio thought about his answer for a while. He couldn't lie to Jackson, who could always tell if he wasn't being honest.

"'S okay."

"That bad, huh?"

"Sir, yes, sir."

"What the problem?"

"Sir, Trainee Rodríguez doesn't really want to talk about it."

Jackson looked him straight in the eye and gave him one of those looks that could freeze an elephant. "Come again?"

"Sir, she's . . . guess she's busy."

"Hasn't written to you lately?"

"Sir, no, sir."

"And why do you think that is?"

Dio shrugged, but then he saw that look Jackson always gave him before he was about to cuss somebody out. "Sir, I don't know, sir. Maybe she just don't want . . ." His voice cracked. He caught himself again. "Don't matter. Trainee Rodríguez don't want her either."

"Lies," Jackson responded. "Don't do nothing you'll regret later."

"Sir?"

"Sometimes you don't get another chance. Trust me."

Jackson's CB radio went off. He answered it, then gave Dio one last look. "Keep your nose clean."

"Sir, yes, sir."

Dio looked at the letter he had clenched in his hands. He knew Jackson was right. He walked toward a wastepaper basket brimming over with garbage and placed the letter on top. Someone was bound to throw it away eventually anyway. He'd have to start a new letter, an honest but not so scathing one.

Dear Jennifer,

Why the hell haven't you written me back yet? I've been waiting for semanas. Over a month actually. You can't be that busy Jennifer. There's no way in hell. You've got me all preocupado. I don't know if you're alive or dead. It's like you don't even care. And you don't give me no real reason why you don't show up for my Visitor's Days either. Even my mom showed up.

What's up with you? I'm trying to be nice. You know how that kind of shit gets me heated. It's disrespectful. We're sup-

posed to be together. You don't know what this does to me to be away from you.

This is not what I was supposed to write. Louise says I should give you "the benefit of the doubt" but I'm being real with you. A'ight?.

I think you ain't being considerate for my feelings. You don't know how you tear me apart and you got me thinking all this crazy shit inside my head like you going out with somebody else, or that something happened to you.

You ought to drop me a note, a post card or something just to let me know that you're still alive.

I've been thinking about you so much, especially lately. I've been thinking about our future and everything. How can we ever make it through if you don't show no consideration? You feel me?

It ain't right. You know? It just ain't. I'm making all these improvements and everything. I'm cleaning up my act and it's all for you. Don't you see that? I got all these plans and everything. And I told Louise and even my D.I. and they all believe I can do them cause I'm doing so good here. But you have me thinking second thoughts.

You have me wondering if I even want to be with someone who treats me like this.

Don't you care for me mija? It's tearing me to shreds. You gotta let me know what's up. All I think about is you all day. And you act like this is some kind of juego. Well I've got feelings too girl. You're not the only one. And I love you. You know that.

So you dog me like that again and that's going to turn on a switch I may not be able to turn off. If I find out you going out

*with that puto Angel or anybody else, I'm going to make you wish
you never met them. Me entiendes?*

Don't do me like this. I need you. I love you. Eh?

Love you Forever,
Dio

Dio dropped the letter in the mail drop and immediately
wished he hadn't. True, it was better than the last letter, but
still, it gave him a sickening feeling in the pit of his stomach.
But what else was he supposed to do? How else was he supposed to get through to her? Yet still he couldn't help but
wonder whether he could have handled it a different way.

Simon strutted through the hall of the main building,
picking up the trash like he always did. His pant leg was
rolled up, just like Dio used to do. He nodded at the members of his squad just like Dio and even said, "What's up,"
just like him.

Simon's eyes darted back and forth as he headed for the
bathroom. For the first time in his life, Simon felt like somebody. He felt like people showed him some type of respect.
It might not have been much, but it mattered to him.

He grabbed a full wastepaper basket brimming over with
trash and was getting ready to empty it when he noticed
Dio's letter.

"What's this doing in the trash?" he asked himself. He

had stuffed the letter in his pocket to drop off in the nearest mailbox when *thump!* Grossaint tripped him.

He landed hard on his face. His nose dripped with blood. Grossaint and his boys were laughing at Simon as he rose slowly and painfully. He wiped his nose with the back of his hand. Simon glared a hole right through Grossaint. Grossaint's smile faded.

"What the fuck you looking at?"

"Nothing much," Simon answered.

His boys snickered until Grossaint shot them a look.

"You think you're hot stuff now, don't you?" He nudged Simon. "Don't you?" and nudged him hard again.

Simon looked like he was getting ready to tear his eyes out, but something held him back, something always held him back.

"You're nothing but a little bitch. That's what you are, aren't you? Aren't you?"

Grossaint whispered something into Simon's ear that melted him. His tough stance whisked away into a puddle of mush. Fear ran through his eyes.

"How'd you like that?" Grossaint said.

Simon started to say something, but an officer appeared nearby and Grossaint and his boys scattered.

Dear Dio,

I was so pissed at you for your last letter. You act like I have to write you or something. I don't have to do shit. I'm doing this for you, not me. Don't act like I'm supposed to do something when I'm not.

And don't threaten me either. You want to break it off? You do what you need to do. I'd like to see you find some other girl that will put up with your bullshit. I've been waiting for you for almost a year. You think it's easy on me? It's not easy on me to be alone either Dio. Es duro. You think it's easy for me to tell people that my boyfriend's in prison? It's embarrassing. So most of the time I just act like I'm single and not interested.

And don't think I haven't been tempted. My cousin's always trying to hook me up. There are a lot of fine-looking men out here Dio, and they're good men too not into all that bullshit you were into before. They've got real jobs and some are even going to school, some are even getting degrees and shit. So don't piss me off or maybe I'll take them up on one of their offers.

I've been going through a lot lately and I've been busy with school, and with dance class and with my family shit and with taking care of your hermanito. So much is going on.

Don't be so needy all the time. You're turning me off. I'm just being honest. I hate when people act like they need me all the time. I can't be there for everyone. I need some alone time too. You know?

And I'm sorry it's taking so long for me to write but if you had any clue what was going on up here you wouldn't even question it. Just give me some time to think about things OK? I'm not trying to be mean or rude or anything. It's just you don't understand sometimes how hard it is for me too.

And I don't appreciate you calling me selfish cause I'm anything but that. I really don't like that.

You don't need me to be happy Dio. You just think you do and you're putting too much weight on my shoulders. I can't answer every single one of your damn letters right away. Who says I have to anyway? I just don't need that kind of drama in my life anymore just like ~~Angel~~ my friends tell me, "I don't need that kind of stuff in my life."

Don't think I don't care about you Dio, because I do. You just got me on a bad day, a bad month really. Just give me some time to think about things and I'll get back to you whenever I can. OK.

Talk to you later.
Jennifer

Dio knew he'd really pissed her off. In fact he'd never heard her so angry before. It felt good that he even got a letter from her, but, of course, it wasn't the letter he was hoping for. Suddenly he felt sick to his stomach. He felt like he was losing her and he couldn't bear to think it. He had to act fast and he had to act smart.

Dear Jennifer,
Baby I'm sorry I said all that shit and I'm sorry you're going through all that shit. You know you can talk to me about things. I know it's hard for you to write back and forth. You know I'd be there for you in a second if I could but I'm stuck here. I want to be next to you so bad. Please don't talk about other vatos with me. I hate that shit. You know I'm the only one for you.

No matter what siempre. Remember? You'll see I'm going to be out of here sooner than you know it. I only have like a few months left. I know you may think that's un chingo de tiempo, but it's going to go quick. You'll see.

You don't know how bad I want to lay next to you, holding you tight. I want you in my arms and I want to kiss you so bad. I miss you baby.

I'm sticking things out here as long as I can. I know it's not easy for you but do whatever you can and please make it for our next Visitor's Day.

Hey, what'd you end up doing for Cinco de Mayo? Seeing as I'm pretty much the only Mexican here except for Simon who's not even all Mexican. I just imagined what it'd be like. And I took un trago de agua and pretended it was a Corona and me and you were at the Fiesta or Spooky's house celebrating. And my arm was around you and we ~~was~~ were chillin' on the couch together. Just me and you, all these people around but we're in a world of our own. Just like old times.

And tell your cousin to go fuck off next time she tries to hook you up with somebody else. I'm worth the wait, you'll see. And things are going to be so much better when I get out. I promise. I know it's hard. It's hard for me too.

I know I'm going to get out of here soon and me and you are going to be together again. I want nothing more than that and I'm not doing nothing to jeopardize it. Know what I'm saying? You're too important to me and I hope you never change. Cause you're perfect just the way you are. And I miss you. And I want to be near you so bad.

I love you so much. I gotta get some sleep. I'm exhausted. Talk to you later mija.

Love,
Dio

It was the Fourth of July and the officers had let some of the trainees go outside to watch the fireworks. One of the good things about being so far from Vegas was that they could see all the fireworks pretty well. Dio's eyes lit up. He was like a kid again. He wondered what Jennifer was doing. He wondered if she was spending time with her family, her friends, or someone else.

Last year they had spent the Fourth of July together. So much had changed since then, so much had happened. If he had known that it was going to be the last Fourth of July together with Jennifer for a while, he would have treasured it more. But how could he have known?

He imagined spending that evening with her. He forgot about all the barbed wire and the other trainees. He forgot about the officers screaming and yelling and all the rules. It was just Dio, Jennifer, the sky, and the fireworks. And nothing was more magical than that.

All the flashes of red and blue brought Dio back to that night, that awful night when everything had changed between Jennifer and him. They had been driving away from Las Vegas forever. It was pouring down rain as the sky emptied its rage on the lonely, bumpy, pothole-filled road leading toward the L.A. highway.

He looked over at Jennifer, who was staring out the window, lost in her thoughts.

"They'll never talk to me again, you know. I thought I was home free, but as I was sneaking out the door tonight, my mom told me I leave now, then I'm leaving for good."

"I know," Dio said, reaching for her hand. "It's going to all work out. We get to L.A., then all our dreams will come true. You'll be near Hollywood and nobody knows me out there so I can start fresh. You'll see. We're almost at the state line; nothing can stop us now."

Pop! Tss! The car swung sharply to the left and Dio realized they had a flat tire. "Shit!" He pulled over, slipping and sliding on the wet road. He banged the steering wheel. Just when things were going fine . . .

They both got out of the car and looked at the tire.

"Damned potholes."

The rain drenched them like wet dogs. Jennifer helped him with the tire. She wasn't about to sit in the car alone, and besides, Jennifer could fix a car faster than any guy he knew.

"This bad," Jennifer said. "Real bad. Wiggie doesn't let anyone get away with nothing."

"We'll be fine. Promise. No matter what, *siempre.* Okay?"

She nodded. He lifted her chin again. "Happy Valentine's Day."

She couldn't help but smile. "Happy Valentine's Day."

"No matter what, *siempre,*" he said with a twinkle in his eyes.

"*Siempre,*" she answered. Her eyes lit up as she saw a car's headlights off in the distance. "Look," she said, as she started waving them down.

"They're not going to help us."

"Why not?"

" 'Cause we're two Mexicans, that's why."

"Don't be so negative. Of course they will."

She stood out in the middle of the street waving her arms about. Dio shook his head, then something bothered him. The approaching car's headlighs dimmed and the car began to accelerate.

Dio could still remember the look of fright in Jennifer's eyes as she realized Acne and Dirty Blond were pointing guns at them.

He dove toward her to get her out of the way, but it was too late.

The officers called everyone inside after they had been out there watching the fireworks for at least a half hour. Dio was making his way back when he passed by a big trash bin. He noticed something moving near it and headed over to it. It was some trainee, digging through the garbage. Dio's eyes squinted.

"They want us to be—"

The trainee turned around, wide-eyed and alert. It was Simon, who looked more like a raccoon than anything. Simon dropped a can of air freshener and stared at him glassy-eyed.

"Hey . . . hey, Dio. Good . . . good to see you, man."

"What are you doing?"

But Simon didn't need to answer. Dio knew exactly what he'd been up to. He'd known too many of his homies who did the same thing. He'd been guilty of trying it a few times himself.

"You know that stuff can fuck you up," Dio said.

"No . . . I wasn't . . . I was just looking for something."

"You think I'm stupid or something? You don't need to lie to me, man."

Simon grabbed Dio by the collar. "You won't tell, will you?"

Dio shoved him off. "Course not. What's up with you? How much of that did you do?"

"I . . . I don't know." Simon giggled like he was from some other planet. "Can't say that I know. Enough." He giggled again.

"Man, they catch you doing that shit and—"

"I know, but you won't say anything, right?"

"I told you I wouldn't. But, man, you only have a few months to go. Why fuck it up?"

Simon thought for a while. "I miss you, man."

"Same here," Dio said.

"Not the same without you. It's . . ."

Simon started laughing, then crying, then laughing again to cover up the crying, and then he couldn't hold it anymore. He was completely sobbing.

He covered his face with his arm and dropped to his knees. Dio didn't know what to do.

"Move over here," Dio instructed, watching for any spectators. Simon obeyed, moving out of sight. He put his hand on Simon's shoulder.

"It's all right, man. You're all right," Dio said.

Simon tried to suck up his tears.

"That's easy for you to say. You got a girl, you got a brother, you got homies. I don't have anybody."

"Of course you do. You got your mom, eh?"

"No, I don't. She don't want me."

"Well, you got your dad—"

"He don't want me either. Told my mom I wanted to stay with her when I get out and she said no. Told my dad, and he said . . ."

Simon shook his head and started sobbing again. Dio grabbed the air freshener can from him and threw it into the trash.

"You gotta stop this shit, Simon. You're going to throw your whole life away, *perro*."

Simon nodded through his sobs. "That's why I'm here, you know. Cocaine, pot, whatever I could get my hands on. My parents got so fed up . . . they turned me in."

Dio sat down next to him. "Kind of was a good thing, wasn't it? Maybe if you can get your head on straight—after all, as Jackson says, 'There are no excuses in life.' I think it's true."

"This is my the second time here, Dio. Second time and my parents about gave up on me. That's why I was crying those first nights when you came, 'cause I don't want to go through it again."

What? Dio thought.

"You talk about all my money like it's a joke. I'd trade it all if I had what you had," Simon added. "Least your mom wants you. She may not be perfect, but at least . . . just do me favor, 'kay, Dio? When you get out, tell your lady I said, ''S up,' a'ight?"

"What?"

"Sometimes . . . I just want to end it all."

"Whatchew talkin' about, foo'?"

"It was me, Dio. It was me," Simon said.

"What was you?"

"It wasn't Grossaint."

"What are you talking about?"

"It was my fault you got knocked back."

"*Chale,* homes, that wasn't your fault. You saw that—"

"No, I . . ."

He was having trouble getting out the words and Dio was getting irritated. *Why wouldn't he just spit it out?*

"I . . . see, I wanted to get out so bad. I can't take this place no more. I couldn't then, but now I really can't. I've got to get . . ."

Dio realized what he was trying to say.

"You did that? You made that hole in the wall all by yourself?"

Simon nodded. Dio felt uneasy inside. If it had been six months ago, he probably would have kicked Simon's ass for what he had done, but things had changed since he'd been in the camp. He thought about things before he did them now. He stopped and thought about the other person's point of view, and though it burned him up inside at first, he soon found that the anger was cooling off, and it was replaced by compassion and sympathy for Simon.

"You ever been someplace so locked up inside you don't know what to do? You want to go, but you can't get out. You go crazy inside, Dio. You go crazy."

Dio thought about all those years being locked in the toy box whenever he was "bad." He remembered all those feelings, calling for someone, anyone to get him out. His tears were for no one but himself because they never did him any good.

"Whenever I could get away, just a few minutes at a time, I'd pull out more and more 'til the hole was big enough," Simon continued. "I just . . ."

"What?"

Dio socked him in the arm. The more Simon talked, the more the façade was fading away. The more the real Simon was coming out.

"*Chale*, homes. You and me, when we get out, you can crash at my pad with me and Jennifer. We're going to get jobs and go to college and . . . and every weekend, you and me and all my homies, we're going to drink Coronas . . ."

Simon cracked a smile. "And chill with all the *jainas*."

Dio laughed. "*Simón, ése*. And play fuckin' oldies."

Dio put his arm around Simon. "We're homies for life, *perro*. Homies *por vida*. Don't let those punks . . . just . . . ignore . . ."

Simon nodded. "Yeah, dawg. They hit me, I got to hit 'em worse, right?"

Dio thought for a while. It was almost an immediate reaction for him to say "yeah," but he couldn't do it. He saw Simon all jazzed up. He had his thug façade back on. Simon had finally become the man Dio had wanted him to be at the beginning, but now as he looked at him, it just didn't fit him. It didn't fit the person he knew Simon was inside.

"Right, dawg?" Simon insisted.

Dio turned away and stared off into the distance.

"Yeah, sure."

Dear Dio,

This is hard for me to say. But I need to do it. The reason I've been in such a bad mood lately and that I haven't been feeling well or getting right back to you is because I found out something from the doctor a couple of months ago. And I didn't know how to tell you cause I didn't want to believe it was true and then I didn't know quite what to do about it.

But I've made a decision and I've got to tell you the reason why I've been acting the way I have is because well, I'm pregnant. And it's your baby.

I don't know if it's a boy or a girl. It's too soon to tell. It's just weird cause I never thought something like this would happen to me. I've always been so careful. I've always taken precautions. It's just weird. I just don't want to be some unwed mother. It wasn't supposed to happen like this. I was getting my life together and things have been going so well. I mean I'm graduating this year and I just got a callback for a new show on the strip. And I have friends now and everything. And I just never thought something like this would happen. *No se que hacer.*

It's just a trip knowing something's growing inside of me and it's got a heart beat and everything and it's so alive. It's so wonderful but it's so scary. I spent the first few weeks just crying about it. It seems like every time something big and good's about to happen something comes along to fuck it up. You know? And I wonder sometimes if I'm destined to fail, to be some kind of poor woman that lives in some shitty apartment downtown or something. I just don't want to be that *vieja* riding on the bus carrying all these *chamaquillos* with her with no father.

Now what am I supposed to do? How am I supposed to ever make it big now? I think I'm going to get this job I have a callback for but what's going to happen when they find out I'm pregnant?

I've even thought about an abortion. But I can't do that. It's too real for me and my mom and dad they'd never forgive me for any of it. Besides you know being Catholic and all.

Mom cried like a baby when she found out and then when she found out it was yours she got pissed! Like you did something to me. But I didn't let her do that. I know I take responsibility too. I should have been more smart.

At the same time. It kind of makes me more determined to make it. Cause I've gotta. I can't be that mother on the bus living in that hole in the wall downtown. I won't do that.

They say the baby's due like around October or November sometime. I'm sorry you won't be out in time to see the birth but I'll send you pictures and I'll tell you how I'm doing.

Just be patient with me okay with the letters? I want to see you too. There's things we need to talk about that I can't write about. And I'll do it as soon as I can. OK?

Take care,
Jennifer

A wave of excitement rushed over Dio and he could hardly contain himself. He was going to be a father, a real father! He and Jennifer were going to have a baby. They were going to be a real family, with a real baby! It was like a miracle. It was like a dream come true, and he had to tell somebody. But who? Nobody in his new squad really knew him. He had never taken the time to connect with them. And he didn't really know his officers all that well. He felt like he was going to explode with excitement.

Nothing this wonderful had ever happened to him, and he knew that now, forever, he and Jennifer would be connected. They had a love child, someone who would be testament to their love forever.

Dio tried to contain himself as he asked his officer if he could use the head. The officer looked at him suspiciously, then excused him. Dio walked as fast as he could, then raced to the kitchen. He knew he only had a few minutes, and if he got caught . . . But it was worth it. He had to tell Louise.

She looked at him with surprise as he tried to catch his breath, the biggest possible smile spread across his face.

"What's going on with you?" she asked.

"I . . . she . . . I can't . . . believe it. It's . . . she's pregnant."

"What?"

"It's mine. It's ours," he said, grinning from ear to ear.

"Oh, my God, that's wonderful! Does she know what it is?"

Dio shook his head. "Not yet. I don't think so. But I hope it's a boy. A girl, a boy, so what? As long as it's ours."

"You're so young."

"Who cares? Lots of people have babies when they're young and they turn out just fine. 'Sides, I'm going to college, remember? And I'm going to provide for Jennifer, me, and the baby. Jennifer and I are getting married."

"You are?"

"Well, of course. Eventually."

"That's . . . that's good . . . well, I'm happy for you. Have you written her back yet?"

"No, but I'm going to. I knew this would happen. I knew a miracle would happen. And I'm going to be the best daddy ever. I'm going to take him to ballgames and to school and to—"

"Wait, wait, don't get ahead of yourself. One step at a time. First get out of camp. Graduate, make a life for yourself."

"I know . . . I know . . . I just had to tell somebody."

She smiled, but something seemed to be bothering her. "I'm happy for you."

"What's wrong?" Dio asked.

She worked up a smile again. "Don't worry about it. You better get back."

"You sure?"

"Go on, now."

"Yes, ma'am," he answered. He hated to see her like this, especially when things were going so great for him. But he raced back to the tent anyway and began his letter.

Chapter Seven

Dear Jennifer,

I about crapped in my pants when I got the news. I am so excited baby. You don't know. And you don't have to worry about anything, porque as soon as I get out I'll work 2–3 jobs whatever it takes to support you and our baby.

I'm going to be the best dad there is. Te lo prometo. That news is the best thing I've heard all year long. It makes me feel motivated.

I've even been thinking about some names. I was thinking if it's a boy he could be Dio Jr., or Luis after my dad, or Roberto and if it's a girl how about Jennifer, or Lupe, or Cristina just like your favorite talk show host.

I knew it was meant to be that we'd have a familia. See? I love you mija. I knew it was <u>inevitable</u>. Know what that means? Learned it from class. It means it's destiny. It's meant to be.

When do you find out if it's a boy or girl? I hope it's a boy. Did you tell Daniel yet he's going to be an uncle? Que dijo?

I can't get over it all that you told me. Wow, I'm going to be a daddy. Wait 'til I tell Louise. Simon's going to get locced when he finds out.

I know you probably can't make it to the next Vistor's Day with you being pregnant and all but I'll be out soon. You'll see. But you be careful I'd rather have you at home safe than risking everything. If there's anything you need you know I'm there for you. You can get a hold of Spooky if you need some money or something and le pago para tras. I'm there for you baby.

I'm asustado but I know things are going to work out. I feel like I'm floating on air cause everything's happening the way I want it. We're going to be a family baby. And I want to have more kids like 2–3 little Dios & Jennifers runnin around. If this one's a boy then I want a girl too to match. Ha-ha-ha! I know, I know one step at a time.

And don't worry about being unwed cause as soon as I get out we can start planning the wedding too. I want to do it at the church on Valley View. You know the one we used to go to all the time when we were younger with Father Martínez?

And you can invite all your relatives (even your mom. Ha-ha-ha.) I don't care I want the world to know, nothing's going to break our love. Nothing. This is the best news ever. ~~Some things happened here and it may take a little bit longer than I expected but~~ I love you baby.

Love,
Dio

Ever since Jennifer's letter arrived, Dio had had an extra bounce in his step. He was more motivated than ever. He didn't just exist when his officers gave him an assignment, he was driven. He told anyone who would listen about him becoming a daddy. Even if they didn't listen, he'd tell them anyway. He made plans in his head and plans on paper of what he was going to do, step by step, as soon as he got out. He started to dream, to dream big. He started to make a list of who he wanted to invite to their wedding, what kind of food they were going to have at their reception, what toys they should get for the baby. He wrote list after list and name after name. He dreamed and he fantasized, the days turning into weeks. Everything seemed to flow; everything was going well for him, everything—until that night.

Simon never was the strong type. Sure, he had a fire inside him, but he never let it out. He kept everything pent up inside and he was destroying himself.

He knew Dio was right about sniffing. He knew drugs had ruined his life, but he couldn't stop. No matter how many times he had been in counseling, no matter how many times he'd been in rehab, no matter how many times he'd been arrested, there was something inside him that just had to have them. He had to escape. He felt like he was drowning in the world of drugs. But he loved the drowning. He loved that light-headed feeling they gave him. He loved hallucinating. He loved how happy it made him feel, like at that moment everything was fine.

He could forget about all the problems at home, about all the times he'd disappointed his parents. He could forget about not being wanted, about being bounced from home to home. He could forget about the future, because if it were anything like his past, he wanted nothing to do with it.

Simon snuck out that night, as he had been doing for weeks now, and went to a back shed area where he had stashed a bunch of stuff he could sniff. He was digging through his pants pocket when he found Dio's old hate letter stuffed in there.

"Shit!" he said, and dropped it in the mail on the way outside.

It was scorching hot for August and quiet, very quiet, as Simon inhaled the aroma.

"What's up, nigger?"

Simon jumped as Grossaint cackled in his ear. He froze, trying to control his breathing. Grossaint and his boys surrounded Simon, and he knew there was no way out.

"I asked you a question, fuckin' coon."

"N-n-n-nothing. I'm fine."

"You don't look fine, little darky," Grossaint said, circling him.

"D-d-don't . . . don't call me that. I'm not. I'm not."

Grossaint just laughed in Simon's face as he yanked his head back.

"What's wrong, Simon? You got a p-p-p-problem? Huh? Huh?"

"No."

"Seems to me you got a p-p-p-problem. Well, I know something that can fix it."

"No. Please. Don't. I don't want to do that anymore."

They laughed.

"Come on, you love it. You always love it."

"No, I don't."

He yanked Simon's head back again. "I said you love it. You want Senior Jackson to find out about your little trips to the shed every night?"

A tear trailed down Simon's cheek. "Please." But they just laughed in his face as each of them unzipped his pants.

"Now do it the way I like it, nice and slow."

Tears streamed down Simon's cheeks as he gagged and did as he was told to each and every one of them. But that wasn't enough.

He spat out what he could, and his stomach turned. They just laughed in his face.

"Come on, faggot. You know you like it."

"I want to go to bed."

"I want to go to bed," Grossaint mimicked. "I'm not done with you yet."

Grossaint grabbed a broom from the shed and broke it over his knee as his boys grabbed Simon. He kicked and screamed until they gagged him with a rag and shut the shed door behind them.

"You ever tell anyone and I'll kill ya," Grossaint warned.

It was Visitor's Day again. Dio, as usual, stood in line as he watched the other trainees chatter with their guests. It was halfway through and Dio just wanted it over with so he could get back to the tent and dream up more plans for himself and Jennifer and their baby. He let his mind wander and drift into space. Then he noticed something, or someone in the distance.

It was some fat girl, no, some pregnant girl waddling inside. Her hair was long and brown and . . . then Dio realized it was Jennifer.

He couldn't breathe, suddenly he couldn't breathe, and when he did manage to breathe, he felt like he was hyperventilating. This couldn't be real. It had to be a fantasy. But it wasn't. She really was there. She was really in the same room.

She froze when she saw him. His whole face lit up at the sight of her. She might have been thicker than he remembered, but her hair was longer and she had colored it lighter and one side of it covered part of her face. She looked more beautiful than ever. He had to restrain himself from running over to her.

She too lit up for a second. She seemed blown away by his appearance. He looked more muscular than she had remembered. He looked healthier. He just looked good, real good. But then she stopped herself and her face became more withdrawn; she could barely look at him.

He took her by the hand to lead her over to a bench, but she pulled her hand away. That should have been the first clue that something was wrong, but Dio was too elated that she was there with him to notice.

She looked around and noticed that everyone was staring at her, all the trainees, all the officers. She turned away. It was too weird for her.

Dio just looked at her for a moment. She was like the greatest piece of art he'd ever seen.

"Your hair," Jennifer said.

Dio smiled, feeling it. "I know. They cut it."

He leaned over to kiss her.

"You look . . ."

She turned away, and as her hair brushed back he saw it, a nasty thick scar across her left cheek. It looked awful. He was shocked. She just looked at him, embarrassed. Something else was in her eyes, anger.

"It's from the drive-by," she said coldly.

Thoughts of that day flooded him. He felt guiltier than ever. He wanted to forget that day forever and have a new beginning, but now she'd carry that scar with her as a memory for the rest of their lives.

"I got your letter," she said.

Of course you got my letter; I sent it weeks ago, Dio thought.

But there seemed more to it than that. Dio hoped that his smile might melt away whatever bothered her; it usually did.

"You look . . . I can't believe you're here. I didn't expect you to come."

She just looked at him blankly. He looked at her belly. She was already getting huge. He started to put his hand on it.

"Don't," she snapped.

"Baby—"

"Don't 'baby' me."

"Jennifer, I know I was a real *cabrón* before, but—"

"Dio."

"No, let me finish. *Por favor.* It's going to get better when I get out. I've told you that. *Te lo prometo.* Anything you want."

She just looked at him. Her eyes burned with anger, then with tears. Her lips quivered. He hated seeing her like this. He wondered if it was just a pregnancy thing. When his mother was pregnant with Daniel, he remembered, she was even more moody than usual. He wanted to hold her. He didn't care about the scar on her face. He loved her and wanted her to know it.

"Baby, please. I'm sorry. I'm different now. I am."

"Time's up," an officer called.

Dio could have just shot him right then and there.

Jennifer gathered her things together. She seemed more preoccupied with collecting her purse and things than with Dio.

"Hey, Jennifer."

She looked at him furiously.

"No matter what—*siempre.* Eh?" he said.

She continued to gather her things.

Dio reached for her.

"Do I get a hug at least?" he half-joked.

She looked him dead in the eye and shoved some papers into his chest hard. Then she stormed off and out the door as fast as any pregnant woman could.

"Jennifer!"

Dio looked down at the papers. They looked familiar.

Then he recognized his handwriting and felt the color rush out of his face. It was the hate letter he had written her, the one he thought he'd thrown away. Somehow it had gotten to her; he knew his world would never be the same again.

Chapter Eight

HE MOPED AROUND THE CAMP FOR THE NEXT FEW DAYS, still in shock.

When it hit him that it had actually happened, it hit him hard. It felt like he had been knocked over by a sledgehammer. He dropped to his knees and felt sick to his stomach—so sick that he puked. He cleaned it up before anyone could notice, but he still felt completely weak.

It was like God was teasing him. It was like God was constantly showing him what he could have, but never giving it to him. He felt anger. He felt embarrassment. He felt hurt. He felt numb.

He wanted to pray, but why? *What good would praying do if it resulted in this?*

Simon never was the same after that night. He seemed more than just in another world: He had withdrawn into himself like a black hole. He had no one to talk to. Dio wasn't around. No one in the squad ever talked to him, and even if they ever did, he'd never say anything. He was always mumbling to himself. His nails were just stubs and he had already started biting the skin around his fingers.

It was almost as if he were a ghost, a ghost that no one could see and no one knew even existed. He was in his own galaxy, his own universe. But that didn't stop Grossaint from keeping a good eye on him. Simon held a secret that was screaming to come out, but couldn't. Grossaint knew it, so did his boys, and they were going to do whatever they could to keep it that way.

They knew they had power over him. Simon would never say anything. He was scared shitless and Grossaint enjoyed every moment of it. They'd spit on him when nobody was looking. They'd make little comments and Simon would just take it until finally, one night, Grossaint puckered his lips at Simon and whispered into his ear, "You're going to be my bitch tonight."

Something snapped in Simon, something that took him over the edge. He took his toothbrush out of his box and began sharpening the back end over and over again against his mattress frame until it developed a sharp point, like the tip of a knife. He kept mumbling to himself over and over again, and everyone kept telling him to shut up throughout the night, but finally the last person in the squad fell asleep. Simon's eyes were dead set on Grossaint in his bunk.

"They hit you, you gotta hit 'em worse . . . they hit you,

you gotta hit 'em worse . . ." he kept saying, moving closer
and closer to Grossaint.

His footsteps creaked against the wood floor, his rage
building and building, until finally he was in front of Grossaint's bunk.

"Die, motherfucker," he said, yanking the covers off Grossaint, whose eyes flickered with fright as Simon swung the
weapon at him.

Quick as a flash, one of Grossaint's boys caught Simon.
But by that time he had already taken a few swings. Grossaint covered his bloody throat with his hand as the rest of
the trainees got up and started calling for Senior Jackson.

Jackson and the rest of the officers came busting in,
screaming on their CB radios, grabbing Simon, who was like
a raging animal. The others rushed Grossaint to safety.

"What the hell's got into you?" Jackson demanded.
"What's the fourteenth general rule, trainee?"

Simon looked away.

"Answer me, dammit," Jackson said.

Simon looked up at him, straight in his eyes, and said,
"Sir, they hit you, you gotta hit 'em worse."

Jackson was outraged.

～

Half of Dio's squad was already out of the tent by the time
Dio woke up from all of the racket. He rubbed his eyes as
he squinted and became conscious of the fact that all of the
yelling and screaming was coming from Simon, whom it

took three officers to contain. He was yelling, "I'll kill you! I'll kill you, fuckin' *puto.*"

Dio was in shock. It didn't even look like Simon; there was someone else inside. For a moment it almost seemed to Dio as if he were seeing himself being dragged away, but he rubbed his eyes again and realized that indeed it was Simon.

The ambulance raced away, as red and blue lights pulled up and they dragged Simon toward the patrol cars. Simon caught sight of Dio and suddenly he calmed. Dio gestured toward Simon for him to "chin up." Simon nodded, his eyes watering.

Dear Jennifer,

They booked him for attempt. 25 years in the joint. They won't let him out until he's like 40 something years old. If he makes it that long. Spooky always told me prison's meant for only the most savage of savages and Simon, even with all his anger, will always be a pussy cat. I'm going to miss him and I only wish you had the chance to meet him.

I was so glad to see you when you came to visit. You looked pulchritudinous to me. Know what that means? It means fine as hell. I'm sorry things ended the way they did. Everyone thought you were fine as hell too. That's why so many of them were staring. They knew my baby was beautiful just like I told them. You're like a legend here. Everybody knows about you.

About the letter, I never meant for you to see that. I thought I threw it out. I was just heated that day. I was being a fuckin tarugo. Louise told me I should write things out, that it's better for me to get my aggressions out on paper instead of directed at people. So that's what I've been doing. I wrote letters like that about my mom too and about other people. I had to or I was going to explode inside.

I never wanted you to see that at all. It was like a journal entry, you know. Baby I want to take everything I said in that letter back. Olvidalo. I didn't mean any of it. I was just pouring through all my emotions, letting off steam. You've got to believe me.

It seems just like every time I think things are going to turn out ~~alright~~ all right for us some pendejada happens. But I know we can work through this cause you know me. Sometimes I say things that just don't make any sense. It's just me talking. I don't mean ~~nothing~~ anything by it at all.

You know I could never hurt you. I'd never let anybody do ~~nothing~~ anything to you at all. And don't worry about any of those cicatrizes and things you got on your face. It'll heal up and if it doesn't it's OK because we can get plastic surgery. We'll get the money together and everything will be good as new. And even if that didn't work, I wouldn't care. You're still beautiful to me baby. You always will be.

We got to stay together because we've got the baby on the way. Do you know if it's going to be a boy or girl yet? No te pregunte.

Baby I need to talk to you real bad. I need you to answer my letters as fast as you can cause it's making me go crazy just to think you might be mad at me.

I need you. And I need to know if you're all right. Please do that for me. OK?

I'm going to be out of here sooner than you know it and we're going to work through everything and I'm going to be a great daddy and a great husband.

You know I don't have no feria here. But I made this ring out of paper clips. It looks chafa, but it's a symbol. I'm including it in this letter and I want you to wear it so it's a reminder of what we have together.

When I get out I'm going to get you a real ring I promise whatever you want. And I'll earn our billetes. I won't be hustlin or anything. I don't care if I have to work at fucking McDonald's all day I'll do it. Me vale. Louise told me they got layaway plans and shit at different stores. Whatever ring you want, you pick it out when I graduate and we'll go out and get it. OK Mija?

I love you baby. Just know that. Just know I didn't mean anything that I said in those letters. You've got to know my heart OK?

I wrote you a poem. Hope you like it . . .

> I loved you
> You loved me
> But maybe I guess
> It wasn't meant to be
> Sometimes I wonder
> If it was just a dream
> A fantasy, a joke,
> that's all it ever seems
>
> But I know in heart and I know in mind
> As days go by and months unwind
> You'll miss me

You'll stop midtrack
And know you loved me
And that, that's a fact.

Love,
Your Soul mate,
Dio

Louise dabbed her watery eyes as Dio read the poem to her. "I'm so sorry."

He shrugged. "Used to it. Everyone who's ever loved me left me."

"That's not true."

"Of course it is. My dad died. Mom don't want nothin' to do with me. Simon's gone, and now Jennifer . . ."

Dio sniffled, sucked up his emotions. He wasn't about to break down, no way.

"Well, forget all that, Dio. Look how far you've come. Look at the man you've become."

Dio nodded. He knew it was true, but that wasn't all that he wanted. He wanted more than that. He'd done all this for Jennifer and now it seemed it was all for nothing. His emotions were bubbling inside him. He could feel them in his chest, making their way up to his face and eyes. He couldn't control it anymore, though he tried to, as his voice cracked with emotion.

"But . . . I want her."

He sobbed, sobbed like he hadn't before. Louise held him close and rubbed his back.

"I know, honey. I know."

He wiped his tears with his sleeve, his nostrils flaring. "Well, I'm just going to have to show her I'm better than before. She'll see."

Louise searched for the right words. "Good."

Is that all she could say?

He broke away from her and said, full of motivation, "She's going to see I'm much better than I ever was and I'm going to be successful and I'm going to be rich and I'm going to make her proud, and I'm going to be the best husband and father she's ever seen. That's what I'm going to be."

Louise just looked at him. She swallowed then looked away. "Good. That's wonderful."

"I am!" he announced.

"I'm proud of you."

But he didn't believe her. "What?" he asked. "You believe me, don't you?"

"I've got no doubt in my mind you'll do that. It's just . . ."

"It's just what?"

"We can talk about it another time."

"You don't think I have a chance with her anymore, do you?"

"Well . . ."

"Do you?"

"Dio, sometimes you've got to love someone enough to think about their happiness."

"What? I am thinking about our happiness."

"But what about hers? Maybe it's not meant to be like

you thought it would turn out; maybe it's okay to just let her go. Let her fly."

"That's bullshit!"

"What? Why?"

"You're the one who said I could do this. You're the one who said I could win her back; all I had to do was just try. I just had to keep my nose clean, that's what you said."

"I know that, Dio. Don't be a quitter. You've got to keep focusing on—"

He grabbed the nearest thing he could find and threw it down, started knocking down everything he could get his hands on.

"You lied to me. You fucking lied to me."

"Hey, don't use that tone with me."

"You're full of shit. This whole place is full of shit. I hate your fucking bullshit stories. I hate your fucking bullshit advice. It don't mean shit to me."

He spat on the floor. "That's what it means to me. You talk about me going after my dreams and doing this and that. You didn't even finish college! You're the quitter. You're the liar."

"Dio, I'm just trying to help."

"You didn't want to help. You're just some lonely housewife who needed someone to talk to."

He stormed toward the door, then stopped, turned to her, and said quietly with a lump in his throat, "I'll send you pictures of us on our wedding day."

Now he felt he had lost everyone. He went to the nearest
private place that he could find so he could just let it all out
and cry. He needed to let it out. He'd needed to for a long
time and it just felt good. It felt good to feel sorry for himself. It felt good to pour his heart out. And although he felt
weak afterward for doing so, he felt cleansed, too. He'd kept
so much inside for the longest time and now it was starting
to get out of him.

"Radigez, get your ass over here and help me with this,"
Jackson said, tinkering under the hood of his car.

"Sir, yes, sir!" Dio said, moving over to him.

"I think it's the starter."

Jackson cleared his throat about a billion times. Dio
knew he wanted to say something, but just wasn't so sure he
knew how to say it.

"So . . ." he started, clearing his throat again, "heard your
girl stopped by."

"Sir, yes, sir."

"Betcha it was nice to see her."

"Sir, yes, sir. It was."

"And how's that going? The two of you?"

Dio shrugged. "Sir, all right. Not too good, sir."

"No?"

"Sir, no, sir."

"Well, that's women for ya."

Dio smiled. "Sir, yes, sir."

"Heard she's about to bust."

"Sir, yes, sir. Sir, she's pretty big, sir."

"Know what it's going to be?"

"Sir, no, sir. A boy? Hope so. Don't know, sir."

"Thought about how you're going to provide for it?"

Dio tried to keep his sigh undetected. He could feel another lecture coming and he wasn't in the mood for one.

"Sir, a little bit, sir. Thought Trainee Rodríguez might work on cars, you know, design shop or something."

"Got any ideas?"

"Sir, Trainee Rodríguez . . . Trainee Rodríguez doesn't know, sir. Sir, who's ever going to hire Trainee Rodríguez with a conviction anyway, sir?"

"Well, that's not a good attitude . . . Course . . ." He didn't know exactly how to put it. "Course, when I was about your age, had a couple of misdemeanors under my belt, too."

Dio looked at him, shocked. *Him? Mr. Can't-Do-No-Wrong?*

"Sir, misdemeanors, sir?"

"That's right."

"Sir, not exactly the same, sir."

"Well . . . it may not be, but when I was your age—"

Dio threw his head back. "Sir, everybody says they know what it's like and they don't. Trainee Rodríguez had it hard, sir. Never had a decent mother to look after me. Been in and out of juvie since I was thirteen. I don't have no money. I don't have no car. I don't even have no lady anymore. How do you think I'm supposed to get a decent job if I—?"

Jackson slipped right back into his drill instructor role. He slammed the hood of the car shut just centimeters from Dio's fingers.

"No, no, and no! I ask the questions 'round here, trainee!"

He stepped right into Dio's face, nose to nose.

"You think you had it hard. Well, boo-hoo. Boo-hoo, Radigez. You know what it's like to wake up three o'clock every morning, just so you can pick fucking strawberries, fucking strawberries with your alcoholic father, just to live every day? Your skin so sunburned and blistered you look like a burned armadillo?"

"Sir, no, sir."

"Well, Franklin in the squad does. Do you know what it's like to be a fucking rape baby, your mother using you like a human ironing board every day 'cause she hates the Mexican that did it to her and she hates you 'cause you remind her of it?"

"Sir, no, sir."

"Well, Grossaint does."

It hit Dio like a truck.

Grossaint was half Mexican?

"You know what it's like to go to work every day, facing the same type of gang-banging loser thugs that killed your son?" Jackson continued. "Every day hoping that you might make a difference in their pathetic little lives and that maybe one day, one day you might save somebody else's son? Huh? Huh?"

His eyes were watery, his lips quivering, though he tried to fight it.

"Well, I . . . I do," Jackson said, trying to cough away the tears. "So boo-hoo, boo-hoo, Radigez. 'Cause just when you think you got it bad, somebody got it worse."

He took a handkerchief out and blew his nose loudly, then coughed some more.

"Think about that day every day. Think about what I could have done to prevent it. Maybe kept him from the wrong crowd, maybe been there for him 'stead of at the office all the time. But there are no excuses in life, Radigez."

He searched his pockets for a cigarette. Finding one, he lit it up and took a puff.

"Now, look what you done did. Got me smoking again." He laughed. "Sit down."

"Sir, yes, sir."

Dio sat right on top of a rock as Jackson cooled off, pacing back and forth.

"You're scared, aren't you, trainee?"

Dio thought for a while. "Sir, yes, sir. Trainee Rodríguez doesn't know exactly how he's going to be a good father. Trainee Rodríguez doesn't know if he can handle it."

"Well, Radigez, I was scared, too. Every new father is. But I tell you one thing, being a dad's probably going to be the best thing that's ever happened to you. Was for me."

Dio looked at Jackson, and for the first time, saw the human behind the shell; behind the tough façade was a father who missed his son—a human being who hoped to make a difference.

"Truth is, sometimes you remind me of him, hard-headed son of a bitch. I loved that boy, was a good boy. Just wrong place, wrong time. Thugs that shot him, all they got away with in the store was twenty dollars. Twenty dollars! Can you imagine that?"

"Sir . . . I'm sorry, sir."

"Well . . . happy birthday."

Jackson tossed him a package.

Dio's eyes about popped out of their sockets as he opened the package and found a uniform. All white, the last level.

"Don't ever say I never gave you nothing."

"Sir, yes, sir." Dio smiled.

"Go on now, get over to your squad. And don't you give up on that girl of yours."

"Sir, yes, sir," he said, as he hustled to join his squad.

"Hey, and Radigez?"

"Sir, yes, sir."

"Don't you tell nobody 'bout me crying, neither, or I'll kick your ass."

Dio grinned from ear to ear, but he knew Jackson was serious. "Sir, yes, sir."

Dio couldn't get to the hooch fast enough. He only wished Jennifer could share his happiness.

Chapter Nine

$\mathcal{A}$ WHOLE MONTH HAD PASSED SINCE HE HAD SEEN JENNIFER. He dreamed about her every night, and it didn't help that everyone in the squad always wanted to know the updates. He didn't really have anything new to say, so he started writing letters to himself and pretending they were from her.

What was he supposed to do? Tell them that Jennifer wanted nothing to do with him? Tell them that he hadn't talked to her in a whole month? Tell them how it broke his heart just to think about it?

Instead he'd write the letters that he wanted to hear from her, the words he longed to hear her say.

"Dear Dio, I'm so glad to see you in boot camp. You looked so good. You looked hot as hell. Just wait 'til you get out. We're going to make up for lost time," he read.

The guys whooped and hollered.

"I'm counting the days until you get out. What, just two more months, right? And I'm getting bigger than ever.

I could pop any moment. I'm so proud of you and I can't wait for us to start our family together. I love you, baby. Love, Jennifer."

"Man, sounds like she wants you big-time," someone said.

"Yeah." Dio conjured up a smile. "For sure."

It was a strange thing, hearing those letters. Sure, it made him feel good to imagine that they were actually from Jennifer, but he hated lying. It wasn't who he was anymore; it gave him this heavy feeling in the pit of his stomach to do it. But he couldn't let the guys down. Many of them didn't really have girlfriends or anyone who cared about them like Jennifer had cared about him. They loved to hear her letters to him. It was as if they were living vicariously through his experience. And what did it hurt if he lied a little, but lifted people's spirits?

He wondered about Simon. Simon used to love to hear letters from Jennifer, too. He wondered how he was managing in the joint. He missed him, *that little runt*. He missed his nerdy little comments, and missed his spirit. He missed how he tried so hard to be something he wasn't. Dio couldn't help but feel somewhat guilty for the whole thing. He was the one who had encouraged Simon to get even. If he could do it all over again, he'd advise him otherwise, that's for sure.

No one had really heard anything from Grossaint since they took him to the hospital. Jackson had mentioned that he had made it out alive and was in the hospital recovering. He'd still have to complete his sentence. Even though Grossaint probably deserved what had happened to him, or at least had it coming, Dio couldn't help but feel sorry for him. After hearing that he was a rape baby, after hearing what a hard life he had had, he almost felt a kinship with him. It was weird, but it was true.

Dear Jennifer,

How's it going? I hope you're doing well. I'm doing pretty well myself. Keeping busy. There's lots to do here that's for sure. All the guys keep talking about how beautiful you were when you came here. I tell them "Of course!" you're my lady.

I hope everything's going well with your singing and everything. I know as soon as you have the baby, your family can help you and I'll watch it too so you can go on auditions. Whatever you need to do I'll be there to support you baby.

I believe in you. It will be nice to tell everyone how I'm married to a superstar. Won't that be great? And I knew you "then." Know what I'm saying?

God we've known each other for a minute. That's for sure. And I'm looking forward to spending the rest of my life with you. Every time I close my eyes, you come into my mind. Your hair, your skin, those lips. God I miss those lips.

I know you're probably busy but I just wanted to say "what's up" again cause I miss you. You're like honey to a bee baby. Once you get a lick, you can't stop. Sounds corny but it's true.

I miss you Jennifer,

Love,
Dio

The weeks kept breezing by, one after the other. Dio still hadn't heard from Jennifer, but he kept sending her letters anyway, hoping that maybe he'd hear back from her.

He hadn't talked to Louise in a long time; in fact, he'd purposely avoided her. He felt embarrassed by the whole thing. Besides, he didn't want to be around someone who didn't support him. She was being negative, from his point of view. What bothered him most, what kept him up tossing and turning at night, was the little quiet voice inside him that made him wonder if what she had said was true.

He kept his mind off it as much as he could. Jackson kept them very busy. It seemed that the closer they were to graduation, the more work he gave them. And he gave Dio more and more responsibilities. He made him lead cadence. Instead of trailing behind like he had at the beginning, he was leading the troop, carrying the American flag as they marched. He was put in charge of classroom groups. He was, for the first time, taking the lead in something and being responsible, and it felt damn good, that was for sure.

When Grossaint came back, no one knew what to expect. Most of his boys had pretty much assimilated into the group. They'd actually become nice to be around, but no one knew what it would be like once he returned.

He didn't exactly look the same when he came back. Sure, he still had the same ice-blue eyes and broad shoulders. And it wasn't just the bandages and the scar he had on his neck. He was just much quieter now, more withdrawn, more . . . human. Or maybe it was just that Dio saw him as more human.

Once Jackson knew Grossaint was physically able again, he didn't let up on him at all. He pushed him just as much as he pushed everyone else, and Grossaint complied.

Dio watched him often—not so much that Grossaint would start to notice or anything, but he couldn't help himself. Somehow, he felt guilty about the whole thing. The more he looked at him, the more human Grossaint became to him. He guessed that he had never spent any time really looking at him that way. He'd always seen the asshole personality Grossaint liked to project.

Dio made his way over to Grossaint one night and their eyes met. Grossaint almost seemed afraid. Dio cleared his throat.

"Um. How's it going?"

Grossaint shrugged. "'S okay."

"You feeling all right?"

"Why?"

"Just wondering."

"Your nigger buddy really did a number on me."

"Hey, be cool, man. I just wanted to check to see if you were all right. And Simon's no more nigga than you or me. He's just as much a Mexican as you are."

Fear flashed through Grossaint's eyes. "Who told you?"

"Does it matter?"

"You're . . . you won't say anything, will you?"

"Depends."

"On what?"

"If we're cool or not."

Grossaint stared at the deck.

"We cool or not?" Dio asked, extending his hand. He held it there for what seemed like an eternity until Grossaint finally took it.

"All right."

Dio smiled. If anyone had told him a few months ago that he and Grossaint would be on real speaking terms, he would have called them crazy. But he guessed Louise was right. Miracles do happen.

⌐⌐

It was Thanksgiving time and Jackson had arranged a sort of Thanksgiving meal. It wasn't turkey and dressing and cranberry sauce or any of that sort of thing, but it was canned hash, Spam, and hard rolls, and even some strawberry jam. Anything was better than nothing.

The whole thing got Dio thinking about his family and how much he missed them. He wondered how big Daniel was, and if he'd even remember him when he got out.

Of course he will, Dio thought. It hadn't been that long. It just felt that long. He wondered if Daniel was staying out of trouble. Dio wasn't that much older than him when he first got jumped in the gang. He prayed that Jennifer and her family were keeping him busy. If only he had had the chance to have someone keep him busy and out of trouble, maybe he wouldn't have gotten himself in such a predicament. It wasn't that he hated everyone in the gang, because he didn't. He had grown to love them. They were more of a family to him than his own family most of the time, but he knew deep inside, even if he didn't want to admit it at the time, that they were nothing but trouble.

It was funny to imagine that almost a year ago, he didn't think there was a way out of the gang life hellhole he was living. But several months of living at this camp had changed his whole way of thinking.

Splat! Dio felt the goosh, hard on the back of his head. He reached back with his hand and realized that someone had splattered jam on him. He turned to see Grossaint and his boys snickering. They had taken advantage of the few seconds the officers had turned their heads.

He's back, Dio thought.

Dear Jennifer,

How are you doing? I haven't heard from you in a long time. I don't know if you had the baby yet but I'm guessing if you haven't you will any minute. I wanted to let you know on this day, and on every day really I think about you always. I think about our time together and how I took it for granted but I think about those days and I play them over and over again in my head.

I miss you. I know I say that all the time but it's true. I miss kissing your soft lips. I miss lying next to you, having you in my arms. I miss the touch of your hands and your laugh, that's what I miss the most.

I've never connected with anybody in my life like I've connected to you. In all my years of living the most special times I ever had were being with you. I don't care if we were sitting in front of the TV watching "Entertainment Tonight" or sitting on the top of the hood of my car looking out at the city. Any time with you was a special time.

You changed my life. You did. You made such an impact on my life that if I died today I'd be a happy man because I'd been lucky enough to meet you.

You're the type of woman, the type of human being that only comes into my life once in a life time. You were a beacon to my soul.

I love you baby and I can't wait to be with you.

Love,
Dio

Louise looked at Dio, then went back to putting the canned foods away.

"How was your Thanksgiving?" Dio asked.

"That was weeks ago, Dio. You're a little late."

Dio cleared his throat. She sighed and added, "My holiday wasn't bad. Yours?"

Dio smiled. He knew she was kidding. "Fantastic. Turkey, stuffing, my relatives flew in from around the country. It was a great old time."

She couldn't help but laugh. "Well, good. I'm glad you enjoyed it."

"Your girls come in for dinner?"

"Remarkably, yes. They did."

"Good."

Dio didn't know what else to say.

"Your hair looks nice today," he added.

"Don't you have to get back to your squad?"

He started to leave, but stopped.

"You have really helped me a lot, you know."

"Huh?"

"You got me thinking a lot and told me what I should say to Jennifer, and I wanted you to know it meant a lot to me."

"Is that all?"

"And . . . " Dio scratched his foot on the floor. "And it was real cool of you."

"Well, I'm glad you appreciated it."

"And . . . I'm sorry."

"Ah, the dreaded two words."

"I didn't mean to be such an asshole. I didn't mean any of the things I said. I was just so . . . I know you don't believe I'll get together with Jennifer, but—"

"I never said that," she said, putting her cans down. "I just wanted you to . . . I don't want you to be hurt. I don't want you to be let down. And I want you to be with Jennifer, God knows I want that for you. I just care about you too much, Dio. That's all."

"I know. Care about you, too," he added.

"Thank you."

"I mean it."

"Well, I mean it, too."

"Any plans for Christmas?"

"Thought about going out of town, actually, for a couple of weeks with my husband."

"So things are turning out okay for you two?"

She smiled. "We're working on it. We're working on it. He ain't perfect, Lord knows he ain't, but . . . you know."

"Yeah, I know."

"How's she doing? Do you know?"

Dio cleared his throat and pulled out a stack of envelopes—all of his letters to Jennifer, postmarked, and labeled "Return to Sender."

"Oh, my God," Louise gasped.

Dio shrugged. "Her mom must have found out she was writing. Didn't let her get them."

Louise shuffled through the stack and hugged him.

"Everything will turn out, you'll see," she said.

"Yeah," he answered.

"I'm kind of glad you came by, actually, 'cause, see . . . I'm leaving in a few weeks, for good."

"What?"

"Well, I got to thinking, about what you said, about me and my own dreams and why I didn't finish college and . . . well, I decided I'm going to. I'm enrolling this January at the community college. My husband's going to help me out."

"Well, that's . . . that's great. I'm happy for you. I am."

She smiled from ear to ear. "Guess I might become a shrink after all." She laughed.

Dio stepped away. "Gonna miss you."

"Gonna miss you, too."

She teared up, but sniffed her tears away. "You can contact me any time. I'm in the phone book."

"Thanks. I . . . better get going."

"Yeah, you better."

Dio started for the door, but then stopped.

"Louise?"

"Yeah?"

"Mind if I call you Mom?"

Her tears welled up again.

"Any time."

It was unusually quiet in the hooch as Jackson paced back and forth, distributing Christmas mail to the trainees. It seemed like just about everyone got a card, except Dio and Grossaint. Evidently, Grossaint's hopes to be reunited with his family for Christmas hadn't panned out. In fact, as far as Dio knew, he hadn't even heard from his brother in months.

Everyone was in a festive mood. It was a quiet mood, but Dio could feel their excitement. A trainee quietly hummed "I'll Be Home for Christmas." Dio stared out the window. Frost clung to the desert; there was nothing but a blanket of clouds in the distance.

Dio looked around at everyone. It seemed like they all felt sorry for Dio and Grossaint because they hadn't gotten anything. Grossaint passed the time by making fun of people with his boys, making little remarks. Jackson passed out the last of his mail and left the hooch.

Wow, not even a card from my mom, Dio thought.

He knew he had really blown it the last time he saw her, but he only hoped that maybe she'd forgiven him by now.

I guess not.

Dio had even written cards for Daniel, his mom, and, of course, Jennifer, and yet . . .

"Radigez!" Jackson called.

Dio looked up as Jackson tossed him a letter.

"I dropped it outside."

It was from Jennifer.

"Sir, thank you, sir."

Jackson smiled as he watched from the corner. He wouldn't miss this for the world.

Dio ripped open the envelope and smelled it. It still smelled like her perfume. He pulled the letter out and a little pocket picture popped out. It was a picture of a beautiful baby girl and a chocolate candy. Dio smiled with pride.

Merry Christmas Dio,

I know it's been a long time since we talked. But I figured it was Christmas time and I wanted you to know that our baby is fine. She was born on November 11th and her name is Crystal Dione Rodríguez. The Dio part in Dione is for you. She was 7 pounds 4 ounces and she's got your eyes. Ojos sonrientes we call her.

You mom came to visit her last week. I've never seen her so happy before. She had tears in her eyes and everything. Wait 'til you see your mijita Dio. She's so beautiful.

I know it's been a long time, but I've needed time to think. For the longest time I was just angry. Not just about the letter but angry at myself for being angry. And angry at myself for ~~moving on~~ some of the choices I've made in my past. And of course carrying the baby, while going to school and stuff hasn't been easy too. But I've been doing a lot of recording actually. We found this studio that's really cheap and even some big time rap artists recorded there. I have a demo now Dio. I finally have a demo just like we talked about. I would have included the CD but I know they probably won't let you listen to stuff there.

Daniel's doing so well. He misses you though. Your whole family does and he even has a calendar in his room where he marks off the days until you'll graduate. It's so funny, like they say out of the mouths of babes . . . We were all at church yesterday for mass. (I lit a candle for you by the way.) And he was all sad and I asked him why and he said cause Desiree's still mad at him. And I said, "Well I know she's my sister but any girlfriend that can't forgive you after all this time, isn't worth it." And he said to me, "You mean like you and Dio?" I was shocked at first, then I laughed. He's so smart. Anyway it seems all is good between him and Desiree. She's forgiven him and they're off to their normal holding hands one minute and peliando over who's going to play with their Playstation the next. God it brings back memories.

Anyway, that got me thinking about us. And for the longest time I've carried so much rage cause to me you had this chain around my heart that I couldn't release. Then I realized I had the key to the lock all along and I didn't feel so bad.

So many things have happened to us Dio. So much has changed since you've been gone. It's like I don't even know that person I was before. It's like I'm a totally different person. My life has turned around for the positive 180 degrees. I'm a mother now Dio, and it's not a hassle like I thought it would be. I mean it's not easy either. I have a lot of help from family, but Crystal brings me so much joy. More joy than singing ever did. I'm not saying I'm

giving up my dream cause I'm not. As soon as I lose some of this
baby weight I'm going out on auditions again. But I've matured
and I know what's really important to me. And now I have more
inspiration for singing than ever.

I know you have graduation coming up and I'm so proud of
you. I guess what I'm trying to say is just like ~~Angel~~ my friends say,
"Sometimes you've just got to realize all the mistakes you've made
in your life and sometimes you've got to just let

Rip! Dio looked up. Before he could do anything about
it, Grossaint had grabbed his letter and picture and ripped
the letter to shreds. He even laughed as he was doing it.

"What the—?" Dio said.

"Was getting bare in here," Grossaint said. "Figured we
needed some Christmas decorations." And he tossed the letter pieces in the air.

Everyone froze, wondering what Dio was going to do
next.

Even Grossaint's boys didn't laugh. He took one look at
the baby's picture and grimaced. "Ugh. It's ugly. What happened to it?" He laughed.

"Give it back. That's my only—" Dio demanded.

But Grossaint tore the picture up, too.

"Fuckin' spics breed like roaches."

Dio's lips got tighter. He squinted. He stormed over to
Grossaint, fuming. Finally he tapped Grossaint on the shoulder and when Grossaint turned around . . . he handed him
the piece of chocolate.

"Merry Christmas," Dio said, and he walked away.

Grossaint was stunned. He opened his hand and looked at the chocolate like it was the best gift he had ever received. Dio swore he even saw his eyes water.

"Officer on deck!" someone yelled.

Grossaint looked up as Jackson got in his face.

"What in the hell is going on here, Grossaint?" Jackson yelled.

"I . . . I . . ."

"Destroying personal property?"

"I . . . I . . ."

"Can't keep your hands off other people's property, can you, Grossaint?"

"Sir, I . . . I . . ."

"I—I—I. Is that all you gotta say, Grossaint? I . . . I . . . ? What's the seventh general rule?"

"Sir . . . trainees shall not touch the property of others without the—but, sir—"

"Sir, I specifically saw Trainee Grossaint tearing up Trainee Radigez's personal property," Franklin said.

"Shut up," Grossaint snapped.

One by one, everyone in the squad repeated what Franklin had said.

"I'll do the shutting up around here, Grossaint. Come with me," Jackson said, grabbing Grossaint by the collar.

It was a little nippy that day, but the sun was bright. Dio stood proudly onstage with the other graduates-to-be. The horns played loudly to a large crowd of family and friends. Dio looked pretty snazzy in his graduate uniform.

All the squads were there, from beginners to the last level. Among the beginners, in a dark suit, Grossaint was forced to watch.

Jackson seemed nervous at the podium. "It's been a long time coming for these trainees. Many of them have very colorful backgrounds, but they've come a long way. Likely farther than many of them ever believed they could. We pushed them, yes, we did, but only to show them they could go beyond what they thought was possible. Beyond their own boundaries to new heights."

Jackson put his speech cards away and looked at them all with a sparkle in his eyes.

"These boys, these men, probably have more fighting spirit than I've ever seen."

Dio was happy that this day had finally come, but he couldn't help but be distracted by the crowd. Jennifer had to be among the crowd somewhere, and he wondered what she was thinking right now. He couldn't wait to see her after this.

Dio held on to his graduation certificate with pride as he searched the crowds after the ceremony for someone familiar.

"Dio! Dio! Dio!"

Dio turned to see his little brother running toward him. He scooped him up and hugged him.

"What's up, little brother?"

Daniel went on and on and on about everything that

had happened that year, but Dio was distracted by seeing his mother smiling nervously. She walked up to him cautiously. They just looked at each other, not knowing exactly what to say.

Dio felt a wave of embarrassment come over him. He felt guilty about everything that had happened before, but was excited to see her.

"Mom, I . . ."

"Sssh," she said, holding her finger up to his lips. She nodded. "I know. Me, too."

Dio smiled.

"I saw you up there, looking all good in your uniform. I'm proud . . ." Tears of happiness filled her eyes. "Never been so proud of you."

Dio hugged her tightly. That had to be the first time he had ever heard his mom say those words to him.

"Thank you."

She took his face in her palms and shook her head with disbelief. "You did it."

"I know." He smiled.

"*Que descanse en paz,* what would your father think?"

Dio smiled with pride. Jackson made his way through the crowd. Seeing Dio, he started for him, but stopped at the sight of his mother.

"Oh. Well, I . . ." Jackson started.

"No, it's okay. This is my mom and little brother, Daniel," Dio said.

"Nice to make your acquaintance, ma'am, Daniel," Jackson said. "That's a fine young man you got there."

"I know," she answered. "I'll leave you two alone for a second."

And she stepped away, taking Daniel with her.

Jackson seemed uneasy, nervous in fact. He cleared his throat about a billion times before speaking. "Nice to see she could make it."

"Yeah," Dio smiled.

"And your girl?"

"Um . . . I don't know. She's got to be around here somewhere."

"Well . . . I'm sure she is. Wanted to give you this." He took out a business card.

Dio's eyes lit up at the sight of it. It said, JO'S DESIGN SHOP.

"Friend of the family. Told her about you and . . . well, you'll probably have to start out sweeping the floors, but—"

Dio couldn't contain himself; he hugged Senior Jackson tightly, then pulled back, embarrassed. Jackson blushed, though he tried to hide his smile. "Well . . . just don't go and blow it. I put my name on the line for you."

"Sir, yes, sir," Dio smiled.

"Well . . . guess I better get moving on. You keep your nose clean, you hear?"

"Sir, yes, sir."

"You ever need anything, you just pick up the phone, you know, and give me a call."

"Sir, yes, sir."

Jackson started backing up. It seemed like he wanted to say something, but couldn't.

"Well . . . remember everything I taught ya."

Dio smiled. "I'll miss you, too, sir."

Jackson cleared his throat and tried to hide his smile, then mumbled something to the effect of, "I'm proud of ya."

Dio spent the next hour or so saying good-bye to his fellow graduating trainees and looking around for Jennifer. Finally, when there were only ten people left, his mom convinced him that they ought to get going. It was getting chilly anyway.

⚯

Bang! Bang! Bang! Dio pounded on the door as hard as he could. He'd spent the last couple of days trying to reach Jennifer at her mom's place, but the number was disconnected.

"Come on, *mijo*! She's not there," his mother called from the running car.

Dio checked inside the darkened windows, cupping his hands over his face so he could peer inside.

"No, mamá. She wouldn't just leave without telling me. Must be some mistake."

"Come on, *mijo*. You've been checking that house for fifteen minutes. If anyone lived there, they'd have come out by now."

Dio knew she was right. It just seemed strange. He wondered if that was what Jennifer had been starting to say in her Christmas letter when Grossaint had snatched it away. Maybe she had written her new phone number, but now he would never know.

"*Mijo!* Now!"

"Yes, ma'am," Dio answered.

He put his hands in his pockets; the wind gave him a chill as he walked down the steps to the running car.

"I don't understand," Dio said.

"They were here just a month ago," his mom said. "Her mom started acting funny once she found out that you were going to be getting out soon. She stopped returning my calls and everything. I don't know, Dio. I don't know."

Senior Jackson was right. They did start him sweeping the floors at Jo's Design Shop, but it didn't take long before they recognized his talent. He didn't mind cleaning so much, anyway. Anything was better than being back in prison boot camp. And besides, he was making honest to goodness, real money. It wasn't the best money in the world, just seven dollars an hour, not exactly like the drug money he was making before, but then he didn't walk around with this dark cloud inside him, either. He could walk away with a sense of pride that he was a responsible citizen.

Dio hadn't been back to his old neighborhood since he got out of camp. His mom had moved to a nicer place now that, what with her new job and keeping sober, she could afford it. Living with his mom wasn't exactly peaches and cream; they did still have their fair share of arguments, but it wasn't like before, not as intense, and Dio was just grateful to have a place to live. Besides, in just a few more months he'd not only have enough to move out into his own place, but he'd also have enough to afford a really nice engagement ring for Jennifer. He knew he'd track her down eventually; it was just a matter of time.

He missed her and was very disappointed he hadn't seen her in so long. He wanted to see his daughter. He wanted them to begin the life he had dreamed of ever since he went into camp. She probably didn't know how to get ahold of him either; otherwise he knew she would have.

He just kept praying. Eventually he knew he was going to have to go back to his old neighborhood. Somebody there had to know where she was.

His boss was a female—a female named Jo, imagine that. And she was a tomboy, that's for sure. She kind of reminded him of Louise, actually. He'd taken a liking to her, and she'd taught him a lot since day one. She often said she had never seen a harder worker. That made Dio proud.

"And that's where we do the finishing," his boss announced.

Dio, under the hood of a car, rolled his eyes and snickered. He figured she was always so loud and was probably taking another client on a tour of the shop again.

"You do rims, too?" a man asked.

Dio stopped. That voice. It sounded familiar. But he went back to work again.

"We do everything," Jo responded.

"Looks like some nigga's car," another man said.

"Hey! We don't allow that talk in here."

Dio froze. He knew he'd heard that voice before; both of

them, in fact. He crawled out from under the car just as Jo stepped up to him with her guests.

"Dio, do me a favor, will you?"

"Sure," Dio responded, wiping his hands, but her voice faded out as he squinted and saw her guests.

It was Acne and Dirty Blond. They had grown more hair, even looked a little cleaner, but it was definitely them. Dio could smell the alcohol reeking from them, and he had to fight to keep himself from gagging.

"It's getting late. Let me get you home," she said to them. "Dio, here's their address. We're fixing their car outside," she added, handing him a piece of paper.

Strangely, they didn't recognize him, though they did look at him funny. He did look different; a little older, a little wiser, his hair more cropped. Dio had to keep himself from exploding right then and there. It was their fault that everything had changed between him and Jennifer. It was their fault that she got shot. It was their fault that he had ended up in boot camp.

"Take my Beemer," she said, tossing Dio the keys and winking.

"Yes, ma'am."

She'd never let him do that before, and for a moment, he was distracted from Acne and Dirty Blond.

"You know where Lake Meade and Skyline is?" they asked.

"Don't worry. You're in safe hands. Dio's our best guy. You can see some of his work over there."

She pointed to a Jeep, beautifully painted with a picture of a sunset with subtle layers of colors that looked incredible.

"He did that. Our hottest ticket. Might end up owning this shop in a few years. You never know. Won't you, buddy?"

"I hope." Dio smiled.

Dio unlocked the doors for them and they hopped in.

"See that they're taken care of," Jo said.

"Oh, I will," Dio answered.

Dio adjusted his mirror so he could see the two of them in the backseat. They were ranting and raving like two drunken lunatics, drinking some beer that they had obviously snuck in.

"Fucking wop, so cheap, couldn't afford food stamps." They giggled as if that were funny.

Acne noticed Dio was watching him and barked at him like he was some little dog. "What do you want? Hurry up, fucking spic."

Dio's lips got tighter. He squinted. He made a sudden turn off the freeway. The two of them were so wrapped up in their own little world that they didn't realize that he was driving into a remote bad neighborhood until it was too late. It had to be the most ghetto part of North Las Vegas, an entirely black neighborhood.

"What the hell are you doing?" Dirty Blond demanded.

"Fucking beaners never get anything right," Acne added under his breath.

"Only thing they're good at is picking strawberries—"

"And grapes."

They both laughed.

Squeak! Dio hit the brakes hard, and they practically bumped their heads.

"What the fuck?" they asked.

"We here," Dio said.

"Here?"

"You dumb-ass, we said Lake Meade and Skyline."

"Me no understand English," Dio said in the thickest Mexican accent he could conjure up. "Maybe you get out. Check see if this right."

"I told you already, dumb-fuck, this is not the right place."

"Me no understand," Dio said.

"I said—" Acne started.

"No, no. Dumb fuck don't understand fucking English. Let's just get out."

And with that, they jumped out of the car, ranting and raving and slamming the door shut.

"Look, this is not Skyline, you Mexican jumping bean," Acne screamed at Dio. "This is some fucking nigger 'hood."

Dio rolled up his window, winked, and took off.

"Hey! Hey!" they yelled after him.

"Who you calling a nigga?" said a deep voice that would have put Barry White to shame.

They turned around and their eyes about popped out of their heads. Five or six big black guys were approaching them and more were on their way.

"You don't want to fuck with me, white boy," he added.

The last thing Dio saw was Acne and Dirty Blond, getting their asses kicked, from his rearview mirror.

⚊

"Daaaaaaamn! Look at you," Spooky said, falling out of his chair.

Dio was decked out in Dockers, a nice sweater, and shoes. He was even sporting glasses. He smiled from ear to ear as he watched Spooky recover from the shock.

He looked around at all the beer bottles and old pizza boxes littering Spooky's living room. Two or three of his bitches were sprawled out on the couch and floor, still knocked out from a night of partying.

He got up and walked around Dio like he was checking out a brand-new car.

"Man, is that you, *ése*? Is that Playboy?" he joked.

"Call me Dio, bro."

"Dio?" Spooky laughed, until he realized Dio wasn't joking. "A'ight, Dio. When'd you get out, dawg?"

"Few weeks ago. Got a job."

"No shit."

"Yep, at an auto shop on Decatur. Only seven dollars an hour, but never know, might end up being assistant manager soon."

"Assistant manager. Damn."

"Hey, where's Little Spider?"

Spooky cleared his throat. "Got shot last month."

"Shot?"

"Didn't make it."

It seemed impossible; he'd known Spider since he was in junior high. They'd all kick it, him, Spooky, Bullet, and . . .

"What about Bullet?"

"Got locked up four months ago."

"Trix?"

"He OD'd just after you got busted."

It was like his whole former world had come crashing down, too. He couldn't help but think that he could have been dead or locked up like them had he been around. Maybe Louise was right; everything does happen for a reason. Maybe being in boot camp wasn't so bad after all.

"Why you all dressed up today, anyway? You going to church or something?"

"No," Dio said, collecting his thoughts. He pulled a little box out of his pocket and opened it to reveal a beautiful diamond engagement ring.

"Damn!" Spooky said. "Where'd you swipe that from?"

"Didn't. Bought it at Mario's. On a payment plan."

Spooky looked at him like he was from another planet. "Payment plan?"

"Gonna check around Jennifer's old stomping grounds. Someone's bound to know where she is."

Spooky turned pale, making Dio nervous.

"What?"

"No one told you?"

"What?"

"Jennifer . . . she . . . about a couple of months ago . . . she got engaged."

It was as if someone had taken a hammer to his head. He had to keep his knees from buckling and dropping to the floor.

"Where? When? Who'd she get engaged to?" Dio asked.

"Some *pinche negro*. Supposed to get married this weekend. I thought you knew."

Dio swallowed. He could feel the tears starting to well up, but fought them hard.

"No. No, I didn't."

Spooky tried to change the subject and hit Dio on the side of the arm. "Hey, we're going to go out for some cigarettes. Why don't you roll with us?"

But Dio was still out of it. *Jennifer, getting married to someone else?* How could she do this? Why didn't she tell him? Why wasn't she honest with him?

Chapter Ten

"DON'T BE STUPID, FOO'. DON'T BE A *PENDEJO*," SPOOKY said, grabbing hold of Dio in his car.

"Just keep the car runnin', *ése*," he answered, jumping out of the car.

It was a Saturday, the day of Jennifer's wedding. It was pouring down rain, as lightning flashed and thunder rumbled.

He tossed his cigarette nervously aside and looked up at the grand cathedral. This whole moment felt surreal to him. It couldn't be happening. How could she do something like this to him?

He opened the heavy doors and felt the rush of wind in his face. The church was crowded, packed, in fact, and the ceremony had already begun. He tried to slip in unnoticed. He felt his jacket pocket to make sure it was still there. It was.

Wham! Dio bumped hard into a glass table with an ice sculpture on it. Bullets bounced on the tile floor and Dio wrestled to grab them before anyone noticed. His thigh was throbbing with pain, but nothing compared with the pain he was feeling in his heart. He'd never felt so hurt in his life. The ice sculpture began to melt.

He weaved his way through the crowd and found a place not far from the front. His mind was racing, so many thoughts, so many feelings. The stained-glass pictures of Jesus and the Virgin Mary seemed creepy to him. It was as if they were warning him not to do it. But he put those thoughts out of his mind.

He knew the risks. He knew he could be throwing everything away that he'd worked all year for. He knew his mother would be disappointed, that his little brother would be crushed. He knew all of that, but nothing was more important than seeing Jennifer one more time and making her understand what she'd done to him.

Dio's nose flared at the sight of her fiancé. Spooky was right—she was marrying a black man.

How could she even think about doing that? He had to be rich. That had to be it. The one thing he could probably never give her, money.

It was a beautiful ceremony; even he had to admit it. It was perfect. It was the hardest thing in the world for him to see it all go on, without him. It was like going out for the lead in a play, a play you wanted to be in more than anything, and then watching it, even though you didn't get cast.

Then he saw her, Jennifer, looking more beautiful than ever as her father escorted her down the aisle. Her dress was white and flowing, with a long train. Everyone let out a little gasp at how beautiful she looked, as she joined her fiancé and the wedding ceremony began.

"We gather here today . . ." the priest began.

Dio's heart pounded. His throat was dry. He checked his jacket pocket again. It felt like a brick against his chest.

"I, Antonio Angel Estrella—"

Angel? She was marrying Angel?

". . . hereby take you as my wife. To have and to hold . . ."

There was a lump in the back of Dio's throat. He wanted to burst out, "No!" It hurt so badly.

"I, Jennifer Lalita Sánchez . . ."

He couldn't believe his ears, she was promising him her life.

Boom! Thunder rumbled and made Dio jump, as the lights went out. Everyone gasped but Jennifer and her fiancé, who were too in love to notice anything. They were illuminated by the candlelight.

". . . to have and to hold, through sickness and health . . ." she continued.

He couldn't help it anymore. Tears came streaming from Dio's eyes. This was too much for him. He was about to explode. His blood boiled.

"With the power invested in me by the state of Nevada, I hereby declare you . . . man and wife."

Dio couldn't breathe. The only thing that kept him from passing out was seeing Jennifer's face as her fiancé lifted the veil. She was more beautiful than ever.

He'd never seen Jennifer so happy. Not even when she

was with him. She really did look like she was in love. *How could that be possible?*

He loved her more than he'd ever loved anyone. Didn't she see that? How could she do this to him?

The ice sculpture melted like it was on fire.

His heart raced as he reached for the .45 caliber in his pocket. He could hear the rain pounding against the stained-glass windows and the roof. His sweaty hands pulled for it, his heart in his throat. He crossed himself, closed his eyes, and prayed he was about to do the right thing.

"Waaaaaaaah!"

Everyone stopped. A baby was crying, Dio's baby, in Jennifer's sister Desiree's arms. Jennifer blushed, then grabbed the baby from her and rocked her.

It was the first time Dio had laid eyes on his baby daughter and it did something to him; he didn't know what. It was like that cry, his daughter's cry, was a wake-up call to him. It knocked him out of the rage he was in, and as he looked at Jennifer so lovingly rocking their baby, she looked like an angel again, like a perfect mother.

Dio sighed. What was he thinking? How could he even think it?

He got up to leave and snuck through the crowd to the back of the church. He passed by the ice sculpture. It was almost completely melted—just like his heart.

Baby Crystal kept crying, no matter how many times the priest tried to wrap up the ceremony.

"I'm so sorry," Jennifer said, interrupting the ceremony. She swept Crystal away in her arms and down the aisle.

Dio was just feet from the door. He put his hands in his pockets and was starting to head out when he ran into Jennifer, who hadn't noticed him.

"I'm sorry, I . . ."

But then she froze. They both froze, just looking at each other, each not knowing what to say. Dio collected himself.

"Congratulations," he said.

"Thanks," she responded. She looked down at Crystal, who had stopped crying all of a sudden, and smiled.

"Say hello to your daddy, *mija.*" She handed her to Dio. She was so small that Dio was almost afraid to hold her, but he did and couldn't help the tears that welled.

"Hi, *mija.* I'm your daddy."

He let her little fingers grab hold of his pinky as he played with her little pouty lips. He smiled and Jennifer smiled with him.

"You're a natural," she said.

He looked at her and cleared his throat. "Anything you need, I'll be here. I want to be a good dad."

"I know. You will be."

They looked at each other endearingly, then . . .

Honk! Honk! Dio looked at the door. He knew it was Spooky.

"I better go."

"Yeah, me too," she said. "Kind of in the middle of something."

He handed Crystal back to her, started to kiss Jennifer good-bye on the lips, but instead kissed her on the cheek.

"See ya."

"Oh." Jennifer fought her tears. From the guestbook on a little table, she tore a sheet of paper and scribbled her new telephone number. "Call me. 'Kay?"

"Yeah."

He started for the door again, then winked. "No matter what—*siempre,* eh?"

She smiled, as her tears welled up. "Forever."

Acknowledgments

SPECIAL THANKS TO GOD (ALL THAT IS) FOR HELPING ME REALize I've always had exactly what I needed in order to succeed. First of all, I have to thank the most amazing kick-ass agent in the world, Jenoyne Adams, who has always been a ball of energy and believed in my book from the very beginning. Without her, there is no way in the world this would have happened. I prayed for the perfect agent who would finally "get it" and to say she's the answer to my prayers is an understatement. There is no one better. The Levine Greenberg Agency rocks!

To my incredible family and friends, especially my little brother, Stephen, who will always be my creative inspiration and those who believed in me from the get-go. To my dad, Lee, for getting up early in the morning every day and going to work to provide for us. I always noticed it and will never forget it, even if I didn't mention it to you.

Also, thank you for those who didn't believe in me, laughed at my dreams, and talked about me behind my back (we both know who you are) because without you I never would have been motivated to prove to you and to myself that I could do it.

To Jose "Dire" Mercado for providing that great book cover design. I wouldn't have had this success without you. To Sergio, Miche, and Andie in Las Vegas for being there at the very beginning. To Rick Gil for helping me make this book as authentic to the Chicano experience as possible.

Thank you also to Cyd Madsen, the godmother of my creative works, for her creative and moral support; to Johnny C. Taylor, who first gave me the idea of turning the *Forever My Lady* screenplay into a novel. To Doug Brown for lending his advice and knowledge on boot camps; his wonderful wife, Tona, for making those great cheesy potatoes they know I love; to the real-life Louise and her son, my late best friend Benjamin Resmann. To the thousands of incredible die-hard fans who made *Forever My Lady* a success in self-publishing and the wonderful online community who made that possible, like Brownpride.com, Chaleonline.com, and especially Sal and Vero at SoyChicano.com.

To my personal cheerleader and proud father, JJ; my close friends Jonelle Ali, Angel Priest, Sam Whitten, Terry Harris, David Meza; Granma Barbara and my late adopted grandfather, Mr. Knighten; my Auntie Jackie Carlyle; Virginia Wilkins; Claudio; Aunty Cheryl who still inspires me; Uncle Eddie for teaching me what it means to create an emotional roller coaster.

Thanks, big brother Ernie and Uncle Louie, for lending me the rent money when I needed it. Foster Boom, Tree, Romina, and "Mum" for introducing me to my personal spirituality. To the many teachers in my life; to Miss Jill Simone Herman, Bruce, and my entire family at the beautiful Ritz-Carlton South Beach for always being so supportive.

Of course, special thanks to my wonderful editor, Andie Avila, and the Warner Books family for fighting to make sure this story is seen by the world. You made my dream come true, Andie!

To Kathy Wilson, who believed in me from the time she met me, when I was fourteen, and mentored me and was patient with me. To the godfathers of my creative works, Joe Wheeler and Ned Barnett, who endured my constant phone calls and questions when I was seventeen but always treated me as an equal. Also to Lenore Baldwin, Daryl Wayne for "the box," and to the beautiful A. A. Lopez—thanks for everything. I'm sure there are some very important people I'm forgetting but just know that I do appreciate you and you know who you are.

And last, but not least, to my grandparents, JoAnne and Horatio Strother, for not only creating the most wonderful mother in the world but also for lending their support in spirit.

Mom, remember when I was fourteen and we had to get up in the middle of the night and clean that doctor's office every night? We've come a long way from living in our car and I thank God every day for having such a beautiful mother.

Reading Group Guide

1. Why do you think Dio was caught up in gangs instead of staying out of trouble?

2. In his letters, Dio insists he would rather work at McDonald's than return to his old ways. But Jennifer became a prostitute in order to survive on the streets. What do you think led Jennifer to make this decision? Did she have other options?

3. Dio and Jennifer fell in love at a very early age. Was it true love or was it puppy love? What is the difference between these two kinds of love? Why do you believe their relationship is one and not the other?

4. Simon comes from a wealthy background, yet he has just as many personal problems as the trainees who grew up poor. What kind of home environment do you believe Simon experienced? Why do you believe it led him to become so insecure?

5. Senior Jackson reveals that he lost a son to gang violence. What do you believe he saw in Dio that began their bond and led Jackson to become a father figure?

6. Louise is reluctant to say much about her estranged relationship with her husband. From what you know of her story, why do you believe she considers getting back together with him?

7. Why do you believe Groissant hates Dio and Simon?

8. Who in your life—whether family or friends—is most like one of the characters in the book?

9. Why do you believe young people should read this book?

10. If you were to recommend this book to one person in your life, who would it be? Why?